WAYS TO GROW LOVE

BY RENÉE WATSON

FOR YOUNGER READERS

Ways to Grow Love

Ways to Make Sunshine

Some Places More Than Others

FOR OLDER READERS

Piecing Me Together

What Momma Left Me

This Side of Home

Watch Us Rise (with Ellen Hagan)

Love Is a Revolution

WAYS TO GROW LOVE

RENÉE WATSON

illustrated by Nina Mata

BLOOMSBURY
CHILDREN'S BOOKS

NEW YORK LONDON OXFORD NEW DELHI SYDNEY

BLOOMSBURY CHILDREN'S BOOKS

Bloomsbury Publishing Inc., part of Bloomsbury Publishing Plc
1385 Broadway, New York, NY 10018

BLOOMSBURY, BLOOMSBURY CHILDREN'S BOOKS, and the Diana logo
are trademarks of Bloomsbury Publishing Plc

First published in the United States of America in April 2021 by
Bloomsbury Children's Books

Bloomsbury books may be purchased for business or promotional use. For
information on bulk purchases please contact Macmillan Corporate and Premium
Sales Department at specialmarkets@macmillan.com

Library of Congress Cataloging-in-Publication Data
Names: Watson, Renée, author. | Mata, Nina, illustrator.
Title: Ways to grow love / by Renée Watson ; illustrated by Nina Mata.
Description: New York : Bloomsbury, 2021. | Series: A Ryan Hart novel ; book 2
Summary: In the summer before fifth grade, Ryan Hart continues to grow
through changes and challenges, such as waiting for a new baby sister
to be born, a summer camp trip, and more.
Identifiers: LCCN 2020053963 (print) | LCCN 2020053964 (e-book)
ISBN 978-1-5476-0058-8 (hardcover) • ISBN 978-1-5476-0059-5 (e-book)
Subjects: CYAC: Family life—Oregon—Portland—Fiction. | Summer—Fiction. |
Pregnancy—Fiction. | African Americans—Fiction. | Portland (Or.)—Fiction.
Classification: LCC PZ7.W32868 Way 2021 (print) | LCC PZ7.W32868 (e-book) |
DDC [Fic]—dc23

Book design by Danielle Ceccolini
Typeset by Westchester Publishing Services
Printed and bound in the U.S.A. by Berryville Graphics Inc., Berryville, Virginia

2 4 6 8 10 9 7 5 3 1

All papers used by Bloomsbury Publishing Plc are natural, recyclable products made
from wood grown in well-managed forests. The manufacturing processes conform to
the environmental regulations of the country of origin.

To find out more about our authors and books visit www.bloomsbury.com and
sign up for our newsletters.

For Madison Marie Hart
Your arrival brought so much joy

CONTENTS

WAYS TO GROW LOVE

1

The Thing about Being a Big Sister

Nothing is the same. Now that Mom is pregnant, everything has changed. Before school let out for summer, Ms. Colby said to my class, "Have a great summer. I hope you have fun and that it's full of special moments. I can't wait to hear all about it next school year." The way summer is going, I won't have any great or fun or special moments to share because all the summer plans we made aren't happening. Well, they *are* happening, but not the way they are supposed to. Mom can't even work her booth at Saturday Market, so Amanda and I won't be there on weekends helping out and walking the aisles searching for trinkets and getting our snow cones. Since Mom and Millie share a booth, Millie offered to sell Mom's products so she can still make money even though she can't be at the market.

This new baby has rearranged everyone's schedule. Today, Mom promised to take me to the library so I can check out some of the books from the summer reading list that Ms. Colby handed out on the last day of school. But now she can't take me because she has morning sickness—even though it is the afternoon. Grandma is on her way to pick me up. She said she doesn't have a lot of time, but she can squeeze it in as long as I promise to be quick.

But who can be quick in a wonderland of words and pictures?

It's not that I don't like spending time with Grandma, it's just that Mom and I go to the library at the end of every school year and we pick out books and have a book club, just the two of us. And every time we go to the library together, Mom points out the books she loved when she was my age and we always sit and start reading one of them before we leave. It's been a whole week and we haven't gone yet.

"I'll go with you next time, Ryan," Mom says. But I know she can't be sure of that. This isn't the first time she's changed the plans at the last minute, and she always says it's because of the baby. Just when I was starting to get excited about having a little sister, she goes and ruins my summer plans. Everyone keeps telling me things will be different once the baby is here, but she's not even out of my momma's belly and already she's changed everything.

Grandma rings the doorbell, and I run to answer it. "Well, hello, hello. You ready to go pick out some books? Got your list?" She kisses my forehead, and I run to my room to get the list off my nightstand. I am ready to go, but when I come back to the living room, Grandma is rubbing Momma's belly. "And how are we doing?" she asks.

Mom sighs. "We are feeling seasick."

Grandma goes into the kitchen, says, "Ryan, give me a minute. I'm not quite ready to leave yet," and she takes saltine crackers out of the cabinet, puts a few on a small plate. "Bring this to your mom."

I put my list down on the coffee table, go into the kitchen, and take the plate of crackers. While I bring it to Mom, Grandma starts making peppermint tea.

We wait for the water to boil and then for the teabag to steep. If we keep waiting like this, I wonder if all the books I want will be checked out by the time I get to the library. Ms. Colby gave that list to all of her students, and I am sure that other teachers gave out summer reading recommendations to their classes, too. If all the rising fifth graders in my neighborhood are going to the North Portland Library to check out books from the lists, I might not even get one today.

Finally, the tea is ready, and Grandma sweetens it just a little with a teaspoon of honey. She takes the mug to Mom, and when she sets it on the table, she rubs Mom's hand and says, "This will help." And she sounds just like Mom when Mom makes me chicken noodle soup when I am sick. She has that same look in her eyes that Mom has when I have a fever or a bellyache or a really bad cold that stuffs up my nose and makes my throat burn. Maybe all mothers look like this when their children aren't feeling well.

"All right, Ryan, ready?"

I've been ready. "Yes, ma'am."

We both hug Mom and say goodbye.

The North Portland Library isn't crowded at all, and I feel bad for rushing Grandma because there are plenty of books to choose from—so many, I have a hard time deciding which ones I want to take home first. Grandma says, "Just choose one, honey, you have all summer to come back and get more. It doesn't matter which one you read first."

"Well, usually I pick out a whole bunch of books, as many as I can carry in my arms. Mom helps me read the first page of each book and then we decide," I tell her. "She lets me check out three at a time."

Grandma skims over the books on the shelf and says, "We don't have time for all of that today, sweetheart." She picks one up and says, "How about this one?"

I don't even look it over, I just say yes since Grandma is in such a hurry. When we get to the counter, the librarian, Ms. Adair, says, "Only one today, Miss Ryan?"

"Yes, just one today. But I'll be back for more."

"I sure hope so. Wouldn't want you to miss out on the Summer Reading Challenge. There are all kinds of prizes." Ms. Adair hands me a brochure that lists all the prizes and the guidelines for participating in the challenge. Then she gives me something that looks like the bingo sheets Grandma and her friends use when they have game night, except this sheet has reading prompts that we can check off during the month. She gives me one for July and one for August. I look them over, and already I know I have to come back as soon as Mom is feeling better because I want to get every box checked. There's extra points for that.

"Come on, Ryan, let's get you home," Grandma says. "Thank you, Ms. Adair."

"Anytime."

On the way home, Grandma says, "I know you're disappointed about not being able to stay longer, but this is all a part of being a big sister now. You're going to have to make some adjustments and sacrifices."

I know, I know.

When we get to my house, I know Grandma must really be in a rush, because she doesn't even get out of the car. She kisses me on my cheek and tells me, "I won't drive off until I see you go inside the house." She never, ever does that.

I get out of the car, thank Grandma, and walk up to my house. Ray answers the door, waves to Grandma, and she pulls off knowing I am safe.

When I step into the living room, the first thing Mom says is, "What adventure are we going on?" and she reaches for the book.

"Grandma only let me pick out one," I tell her.

Mom rubs her belly. "We'll get more, sweetheart. We will."

"I hope so, because I want to win!" I show Mom the Summer Reading Challenge bingo sheets.

Mom hardly even looks at them. She smiles. "Every time you talk, the baby kicks."

"Really?" I ask.

Mom takes my hand and places it on her belly. And then I feel my baby sister waving hello.

"She's moving, she's moving!"

"I know," Mom says. "She must like your voice."

I sit on the sofa next to Mom, tuck my feet under myself, and get real close. My baby sister likes the sound of my voice. I don't know if I will ever stop smiling over this.

The thing everyone tells me about being a big sister is that I'm going to have to share and sacrifice, and help out more, and live up to my name by being a leader and setting an example. But no one told me anything about how it would feel the first time I put my hand on my mom's belly, that I would feel my little sister waving hello. No one told me how it would feel to know that my baby sister already wants to play with me. I want to play with her too, and hold her, and teach her all the things I know. And so even though she's the reason Mom couldn't come with me to the library, and even though she's the reason so much is changing, changing, I snuggle up close to Mom, open my book, and start reading out loud, and take my mom and my baby sister on an adventure.

Oaks Park

2

I<small>T'S</small> <small>SUNDAY AND DAD</small> doesn't have to work tonight, so we're having a family outing. Every summer we go to Oaks Park and ride as many rides as we can and roller skate at the rink, and at the end of all the spinning and twisting and whirling and rolling, we eat burgers and french fries from the concession stand and we end the day with root beer floats—and I am usually so full and tired by the end of it all that I fall asleep in the car on the way home. This summer, we're still going to Oaks Park, but everything feels different.

Mom says, "I've packed some snacks for us that

we'll have in case we get hungry while we're out. We'll have dinner here at the house, once we get back."

And I know this means there is not enough money for burgers and fries and root beer floats, but at least we're still going. And at least we'll still get the Classic Ride Bracelet that means we'll have unlimited times to get on any of the classic rides, plus we each get a ticket to roller-skate for one hour.

When we get to Oaks Park, we stand in line to pay our admission. Mom says, "So, Ryan, you and Ray will go with Dad and get on all the rides you want. I'll be in the arcade, okay?"

"But why aren't you riding the rides with us?" I ask. Mom loves the Ferris wheel because of the views of Portland's west hills and the Willamette River.

"Pregnant women can't get on rides, sweetheart."

"So you're not riding any of the rides?" Ray asks.

"Not this time," Mom says.

This baby. Always ruining the plans.

"I'll watch you a little bit, take a few photos if I can

get a good shot, and then I'll go have some fun of my own."

"That doesn't sound fun at all," I tell Mom. Who comes to Oaks Park to play video games by themselves?

"I'll be fine. The arcade has all the vintage games I played when I was your age." We step up to the counter, pay, and get our bracelets. Mom has a different color than me, Ray, and Dad since she is only going to the arcade.

Because it's the weekend, it is crowded and the lines are long. "Pick your pleasure. What ride do you want to get on first?" Dad asks.

"The Tree Top Drop!" says Ray.

"The Carousel!" I say

Ray shakes his head in protest. "Carousels are for babies."

"No they're not, Ray. Shut up!"

"Hey—we don't say *shut up*, remember? And Ray"—Dad gives Ray a stern look—"get it together or we'll just go home right now."

I point to the Carousel and say, "I only said let's do that first because it has the shortest line."

"Because it's for babies," Ray mumbles. He's really good at whispering something so only I can hear, so if I tattle there's no proof of what he said.

"Good point, Ryan," Mom says. "Let's go to the Carousel first since it has the shortest line."

We wait for the ride to finish up before it's our turn. The horses move up and down, up and down, and each one is decorated differently. Mom tells us the Carousel was built in 1912 and that she used to ride it with Grandma and Aunt Rose when she was a little girl. "But your grandma would sit on one of those benches," Mom says, pointing to the two benches that face each other. They look like a sleigh and have horses painted on the sides.

"That's where I'll be," Dad says. "Which horse do you want, Ryan?"

"That one!" I point to the horse that is painted black with bright sky-blue lines zigzagging across it. Its mane and tail are white.

"And what about you, Ray?"

"I'm not going to get on this one. I'll wait for the next ride," Ray says. Then he mumbles again, "Because I'm not a baby," and gives me a look, but I don't care. I'm getting on the Carousel, and I'm going to ride the black horse. When it's time to board the Carousel, Dad and I show our wristbands and get on. I circle the ramp, looking for the black horse.

There's a girl and a woman walking in front of us. Every time the woman asks, "What about that one?" the girl shakes her head and keeps walking. She is passing up all the horses, and I am beginning to think that maybe she is looking for the black one just like I am.

I walk faster, but I can't pass her because there isn't that much space. Just when I see the black horse, I tug on Dad's arm. "There it is! There it is!"

The girl stops, and my heart sinks. Is she really about to get on my horse? She touches the pink and gold one and says, "This one, Mom. I want this one." Her mom helps her get on.

I take a deep breath.

Dad helps me climb onto my horse and gets me buckled in. "I'll be right there," he tells me, pointing at the sleigh.

"Okay." From here, I can't see Mom or Ray, but as soon as we start moving, I see them. I wave to them as Mom takes a picture. We go round and round, at first kind of slow but then it speeds up and I imagine myself riding a horse in a field, galloping up hills as the wind tickles my face. Every time I see Mom, I wave to her. But the last time she is not standing there. Ray is still there, though. Looking bored and not paying attention to me at all. He misses me waving, and now the ride is coming to an end.

We slow down, down, down to a stop. I get off the horse, wait for Dad to come to me, and we walk off the carousel. "Where's Mom?" I ask Ray.

"She got tired of standing," Ray tells us. "She went to find a seat where the picnic tables are." He points toward the waterfront.

Dad hurries over to Mom, and Ray and I follow.

On the way, Dad says, "Maybe this wasn't a good idea to have your mom out here in this heat."

I see Mom sitting on the edge of a bench, her back leaning against the table. She is drinking out of her water bottle and eating one of the peanut butter and jelly sandwiches she packed for us. Dad sits next to her. "You okay? Should we leave?"

"I'm fine. We just needed to rest." Mom rubs her stomach. "I'm actually enjoying just sitting and people-watching." Mom digs in her bag and grabs a small container that is filled with baby carrots. She munches and crunches. "You all go ahead. I'm going to sit right here. I'm fine."

"But you're not even going to play your favorite arcade games?" I ask.

"Not this time, Ryan. We are too tired."

Every time she says *we* she rubs her belly, and I just don't know how to feel about my baby sister who sometimes makes me so happy and other times makes me so frustrated.

Dad and Mom do that thing that adults do when

they are talking with their eyes, not saying any words at all but having a whole conversation. Dad says, "Okay. We'll just do four rides. Ray can choose two, Ryan can choose two. No skating."

"But Dad!" I cross my arms. What's the point of having unlimited bracelets if we're not going to ride as much as we want?

"Ryan, pick two rides," Dad says, and the tone in his voice tells me not to test him.

Ray says, "This isn't fair. Ryan already chose one. The baby Carousel ride."

"Ray and Ryan, fix your attitudes. Now." Dad stands but he doesn't start walking, he just stands there waiting for us to get it together.

I touch Mom's belly. "Feel better, Mom."

"Yeah, I hope you feel better, Mom," Ray says.

We walk away with Dad, and we switch back and forth, Ray first choosing to ride the Tree Top Drop, which is exactly what it sounds like—a freefall, then up again, then fall again, then up and fall and up and fall, and even though I am scared to get on, I do not tell either of them because I am not going to give Ray another reason to call me a baby.

The Tree Top Drop isn't so bad. I kept my eyes closed, though. And Ray, who says he's not a baby, sure did scream a whole lot. Loud. Next, I choose the Spider, and Ray is happy about that because he wanted to ride that, too. We spin and stop, spin and drop, and when I get off, I really just want to ride again, but I know we have to get back to Mom.

"Let's do the Cosmic Crash!" Ray says. But when we walk over to the entrance, we realize the line is way too long. I guess everyone loves bumper cars as much as we do.

"I think we have time for one more," Dad says.

"Let's go on the Ferris wheel," Ray says. It feels kind of weird going without Mom since it's her favorite. Mom and I usually ride it together while Dad and Ray are doing something else. But today, it's me and Dad and Ray. The seat is big enough for the three of us. Dad sits in the middle, and we buckle ourselves in. We take off into the sky and dangle in the air and round and round we go, higher than the tops of the trees.

The last time around is slow and then we stop. It takes a while for it to be our turn to get off. Once we're off, Dad calls Mom. I hear him say, "Yeah, they're good. No problems at all." Mom says something and then he says, "Are you sure?" And then he says, "Oh, good idea. Okay." Dad hangs up, and I pretend like I haven't been listening and like I don't want to ask what's going on. "We're going to have lunch here in the picnic area," Dad tells us. "But first, let's get something cold and sweet to cool us down."

Ray and I look at each other and smile. We might not be getting cheeseburgers and fries today, but we are getting our root beer floats. Not everything has changed.

Splash

3

Amanda has come over today. She's with me, KiKi, and Ray, riding our bikes to Alberta Park so we can meet up with Aiden and Logan. Ray says, "I found a shortcut, follow me." And he pedals fast, turning at the corner. But instead of going straight to the end of the block, Ray turns right into what I think is a driveway at first, but then I realize it's an alley. It's kind of like a hidden street tucked away in the middle of the block. "Isn't this cool?" Ray shouts. "It's a whole maze back here."

We ride through connected alleys, and I pretend that we are in tunnels and no one can see us. Being on the backside of people's houses is kind of strange because I am used to only seeing the front, where everything looks more put together: flower pots on porches, freshly cut grass, trimmed hedges. But the parts no one can see aren't that pretty at all. This is where the garbage cans are, and bikes with flat tires, and rusting tools, and stray cats wandering around.

"Turning left," Ray calls out. And then we are across the street from the park.

"Whoa. That was fast," KiKi says.

"Super fast," Amanda says.

"We should come this way all the time." I can see Aiden and Logan at the park with Aiden's older cousin, Megan. She watches him during the summer while his parents are at work and so she kind of takes care of us all since we play together just about every day.

We say our hellos, and Megan hugs us girls. She rubs the top of Ray's head and says, "What's up? Y'all ready for a fight?" She is laughing and points to a cooler that is sitting under a tree next to a beach bag stuffed with towels.

Logan opens the cooler. "I'm soaking everybody!"

He takes out a water balloon and pretends to throw it at KiKi, but it doesn't leave his hand.

KiKi takes out two balloons. "Oh, I bet you can't get me."

"Hold on, hold on," Megan says. "There are rules. Actually, it's not a free-for-all water balloon fight. I thought it would be fun to play dodgeball but with balloons."

Aiden says, "Boys against girls?"

"So you can lose?" Amanda says.

"Whatever," Rays says. "If we play boys versus girls, you three will be soaked and all of us will be dry."

"Dry? You don't think we can even get in a few hits?" I ask. I look at KiKi and Amanda, and we all just shake our heads.

"Okay, well first—a few rules," Megan says. Aiden sucks his teeth. "Who has rules for fun?"

"We do," Megan says. "No throwing at someone's face. If anyone is standing here, touching this tree, they are in the dry zone and can't get hit."

"Each team gets a point for hitting someone on the opposite team, right?" Aiden asks.

"Yes, and I will keep points," Megan says.

"All right, let's do this." Ray pulls two balloons out of the cooler and walks a short distance away, far enough to be out of the dry zone but close enough to run back for more ammunition.

We all get in line. Girls on one side, boys on the other.

I am holding three balloons. Two in my left hand, one in my right.

"Ready?" Megan shouts.

And we begin. I make the first hit—getting Aiden as he's charging for KiKi. Logan gets me back. A balloon splashes against my leg just as I throw one at Ray. I get him! Amanda is hit on the side of her arm as she's running back to the dry zone. I think it came from Logan.

Aiden, who is taking this so seriously, slips and falls as he aims for me. I jump out of the way, and the balloon falls on top of the grass. I can't believe it doesn't burst open. I pick it up and throw it at Aiden. I have to pull my arm way back and throw with a lot of force because I am too far away for it to hit him if I just throw it soft. It glides through the air, and Aiden doesn't even see it coming. He is too focused on drenching Amanda. It hits him right in his chest.

Splash!

I run over to the dry zone and call Amanda and KiKi to come over to help me gather up the rest of the balloons. There aren't that many left, but there are too many for me to carry in my hands. I pull my shirt out, making a pouch like I'm a kangaroo. "Stuff my shirt with the rest of the balloons and let's attack them."

The boys don't realize I'm taking all the balloons at first because my back is to them. Once I turn around, they see us running to the game zone, and Aiden yells, "No fair! You can't hog all of the balloons!"

As soon as he says it, KiKi hits him on his right shoulder. Amanda has two balloons in her hand, one

24

for Ray and one for Logan. She misses hitting Logan because he ducks down, but KiKi is already on him and she gets him. *Splash!*

Aiden runs over to the dry zone, searching the cooler. "They took them all? No fair."

"Nothing in the rules against building a strategy," Megan says.

"Well, I'm staying in the dry zone," Aiden says. He calls for Ray and Logan to join him, and they think that's going to help them not lose, but as they run toward the dry zone we chase them, hitting them one after the other and laughing the whole time.

Splash!

Splash!

Splash!

The boys stand under the tree, soaking wet.

Megan takes the beach bag and hands out towels.

"That was a great game," she says. "I hate to admit this, but I lost track of points."

"Oh, it's okay," I say. "It's clear who won—just look at the driest team."

All us girls are laughing, but the boys are sore losers. Ray says, "Only because you cheated."

"We didn't cheat. We were just better thinkers than you," KiKi says.

We all dry off and of course the boys want a rematch, but since there are no more balloons, we promise to do it again later this summer. We stay at the park and play on the tire swings, slides, and merry-go-round.

I could play all day with KiKi and Amanda, but I know we can't stay outside forever. It is so hot that by the time we ride our bikes home we have dried off completely. We turn down KiKi's block, and she rides her bike into her driveway. "See you tomorrow," she says, waving and balancing herself.

Amanda's mom is already waiting when me, Amanda, and Ray get home. Ray and I put our bikes in the garage and say goodbye to Amanda.

Ray opens the screen door to go into the house.

I'm not ready to go inside. Now that it's summer, Dad put two rocking chairs on the porch. He bought them at a yard sale. Sometimes I sit out here and read, and sometimes I just daydream, rocking back and forth and thinking about how soon my baby sister will be here and how one day, we'll be playing on this porch pretending it's a stage, or a spaceship, or whatever she wants it to be.

I sit in one of the rocking chairs.

"You're not coming in?" Ray asks.

"Not yet."

"You're just going to sit there?"

"Yeah."

Ray goes inside, the screen door slams because he never, ever closes it gently. I hear Mom fuss at him. I sway back and forth in the rocking chair and then Ray comes back outside, carrying a small bottle of bubbles. He hands it to me and sits in the other rocking chair. He rocks, back and forth, catching my rhythm. We are in sync like our chairs are a mirror of each other. I blow bubbles into the summer sky; they float and hover near us, then disappear. Ray says, "That was a really good strategy today."

I smile. "I know."

4

A Pickle is a Fruit, a Pickle is a Vegetable

Dad works the night shift, so that means he usually comes home around six thirty in the morning. While we are all waking up and starting our day, he is going to bed and sleeping. Mom is on bed rest. It doesn't mean she has to stay in the bed all the time, but she can't do all the things she normally does. She has to take it easy. So I make breakfast for the two of us. Ray usually just eats a bowl of boring cereal, which is fine with me because I don't need his remarks about if what I'm making is too spicy or too cheesy or too whatever he doesn't like.

I try to come up with something different every day. Yesterday, I made blackberry yogurt parfaits with clusters of granola throughout the glass jars. Today, I'm making toast with peanut butter spread across every inch of the bread with banana slices on top. Grandma promised that this weekend she'll teach me how to make omelets. She is coming over more and more since Mom can't do much. She says we have to make sure Mom is resting and that we need to help out as much as we can.

After breakfast, I read a little in my room and then KiKi calls and asks to come over. We hang out in my bedroom, listening to music. KiKi is standing at my dresser looking in the mirror, striking different poses to the beat, teaching me her moves. When the song is over, she stops dancing and picks up the canister that's sitting on my dresser. "You still think this thing is haunted?" she asks. She pulls the lid off and takes everything out: two seashells, a postcard addressed to no one, a white handkerchief, dried rose petals, and three gold hairpins.

"Not really, but I still want to know why the person who lived here before me left this here," I tell her.

"I've been saving money so that the next time I go to Saturday Market I can buy the missing one from Ms. Laura. Make the whole set complete." Grandma has chores for me to do at her place, so hopefully by the end of summer I'll have enough to buy the hairpin. I just hope it's still there.

"I wonder why people keep things like this. None of this stuff seems special at all."

KiKi puts the keepsakes back into the canister.

"Let's go outside. We can finish making up our dance routine. There's more room in your backyard."

She says *our* dance routine, but really she is the one making up all the moves because KiKi is great at dancing. I'm just good. We go out the back door and have the whole backyard to ourselves. The grass isn't as green as it was at my old house, but Dad says he's going to work on that and make sure he gets the yard looking good. Mom is thinking about planting a garden so I can have ingredients for my recipes right at my fingertips.

We spend the rest of the afternoon making up a dance routine to one of our favorite songs. KiKi plays it off her cell phone, turning up the volume as loud as it goes. "Okay, and then we go like this," KiKi says. I copy her movement.

"No, like this." KiKi lifts her hands and twirls, and I'm pretty sure that's exactly what I did.

I try again.

"Um, okay, how about this instead?" Kiki does another move, and I think this is her way of telling me I am not that good at dancing. She replays the song, and we do our dance routine as if we're performing in a big stadium—something I would never, ever do, but it's fun to pretend.

The sun is beaming down. We go inside for something to drink. The screen on the back door slams, and Mom calls out to us, "Careful with that door. You'll wake your father."

"Sorry," we both say at the same time.

We guzzle down our glasses of lemonade and rush back outside.

"Want to dance to another song?" Kiki asks.

"It's too hot to dance," I say. And besides that, I don't have good coordination, so maybe we should play something else.

"Let's play Do You See That?" KiKi walks over to the wicker basket on the back porch. It's full of outdoor blankets that we never use in the house. She grabs one of the blankets and spreads it on top of the grass, and we lie on our backs looking up at the clouds. The fluffy clusters are bundled together, floating in the sky. "I see a rocking chair. Do you see that?" KiKi asks.

I search the sky for the figuration KiKi sees. I look and look but don't see any clouds that are in the shape of a rocking chair. Then, at the right corner of the sky, I see it. "Yes, I see a rocking chair! I also see a woman smiling. Do you see that?"

Right away, KiKi says yes, like we were looking at the same exact spot. We keep the game going, looking up at the sky, searching for cloud-pictures. We've spotted a shoe, an arrow, a frown, and a giant hand open wide reaching down. KiKi sees a heart, but no matter how hard I try to find it, I can't.

The clouds shift and a breeze blows, cooling us down for just a moment. KiKi kicks her sandals off.

"Have you registered for church camp yet?"

"Not yet. But I will."

"I just did yesterday," KiKi tells me.

I turn to face her. "You put me down to be your cabinmate, right?"

"Of course."

"Okay, good. Just double-checking," I say. "Amanda's coming, too."

"She is?" KiKi turns on her side, leans on her arm. "We're going to have so much fun. We all have to be in the same cabin. It'll be like our own slumber party three nights in a row."

"I know. I can't wait." I say.

Every July my church has summer camp. Campers stay for three days and nights, and return home on the fourth morning. Ray has gone for the past two years. Now that I will be in the fifth grade, I get to go.

I can't wait to hike the trails, learn new songs, and stay up all night talking with KiKi and Amanda. Amanda used to go to our church, too, but ever since her family moved to Lake Oswego, they've been attending a church closer to their home. Everyone will be so happy to see her; it will be just like old times.

KiKi leaves before dinner. When I go inside the house, Dad and Mom are in the kitchen. Dad is putting away jars of pickles into the pantry. "This is really getting out of control," Mom says. Her hand is on her hip, and she is shaking her head.

For the past three weeks Dad keeps bringing jars of pickles home because one of his co-workers believes that pregnant women crave them. Every other day, his co-worker gives him a jar and says, "Give this to your wife," and Dad doesn't ever say, "No thank you," so our cabinets are full of jars of pickles.

"Please don't come home tomorrow morning with another jar. We're running out of space to store them," Mom says.

"I'm making room in the pantry," Dad says.

"I don't need you to make room for more. I don't want more pickles. I don't even want the ones we have!" Mom gives Dad the look she gives me and Ray when we are getting on her nerves. This is not good. Mom is supposed to be taking it easy, not arguing about pickles.

Dad should probably be agreeing with Mom, but instead he says, "Well, he's just trying to help. I can't tell him to stop giving them to me. I don't want to be rude."

They go on and on about the pickles. Mom says, "They're just going to go to waste. And you know I don't like wasting food. It doesn't make sense to keep taking them if no one is eating them. Someone needs to eat these pickles," Mom says. "And it's not going to be me. I don't even like pickles. Just looking at them turns my stomach upside down."

Dad ends the argument by saying okay, and when evening comes, we do our usual routine of brushing teeth and saying prayers and *I love yous* and *sleep tights*.

Soon, Dad will leave for work and the house will feel empty without him.

When Mom and Dad close my door, it takes me a long time to fall asleep and once I do get to sleep, I don't sleep that long. I wake up thinking how upset Mom was about those pickles. When she wakes up in the morning, those pickles will still be in the jars and I don't want her to get upset all over again. Grandma says it isn't good for a woman carrying a child to be stressed. She says stress isn't good for the baby. And I don't want my little sister to feel bad while she's waiting to meet us. I don't want her feeling anything but all the love that's waiting for her.

I get out of bed real, real quiet and tiptoe to the kitchen. I stand on a stool and pull out each jar from the cabinet. I think up a solution that won't waste any of the pickles.

I decide to eat *all* of them.

I twist the lid until it makes a popping sound and then I sit on the floor, and one by one I eat the fat, juicy pickles. I am on my fourth one when Ray comes into the kitchen, rubbing his eyes. He stares at me sitting here on the tile floor, with a jar of pickles in front of me and a half-eaten one in my hand. "I'm telling!" he warns.

"Telling what?"

"That you're in here sneaking food."

"Shh! I'm not sneaking anything," I whisper. "I'm making sure Mom and Dad don't fight tomorrow." Ray sits on the floor across from me. "What do you mean?"

I tell him all about Mom and Dad's argument and how Mom said somebody better eat these pickles. And how she seems really stressed and how stress isn't good for our baby sister and that I think we should do something because Grandma said we have to keep Mom happy so she has a happy, healthy baby.

"But you can't eat all of them by yourself," Ray says.

I scoot an unopened jar closer to him.

He sighs, twists open the jar, and takes a pickle out.

All night long we sit and eat pickles, opening jar after jar as quietly as we can. I have stopped counting how many I've eaten but I know my stomach is hurting. "I don't feel good," I tell Ray.

"Me neither." He closes the lid to his jar. "Do you think the pickles are making us sick?"

"No," I tell him. "Pickles are vegetables. Vegetables can't make you sick."

Ray looks at me full of doubt. "I thought pickles are fruit."

Maybe he's right. "Well, even if they are—fruit is good for you. There's no such thing as eating too much fruit or vegetables." As soon as I say this, my tummy twists. "I think I'm full," I say.

"Me too."

I look at the jars and I realize that most of them are empty of the pickles but not the juice. "I know what we can do." I stand up and go to the cabinet that has plastic ice trays that we hardly use because our freezer has an ice maker. "We can pour the juice in these like Mom does when she makes juice cubes for smoothies."

Ray gets up and joins me at the counter. "I've never heard of pickle smoothies."

"Maybe they taste good. Dad loves smoothies. He'll drink it. And even if he doesn't, we can melt them when we're ready to use them like Mom does in the winter for soup." I've helped Mom make her winter soups. Sometimes she makes more than enough and we pour the extra stock in ice cube trays and save them for later. I get a stool so I am high enough to pour the pickle juice neatly into the trays. Ray helps.

"What about this one?" he asks. There's one more jar of pickles that hasn't been opened.

We are out of ice trays, and I really don't want Mom to see even a trace of pickles in the kitchen tomorrow when she wakes up. I sit back down on the kitchen floor, twist the top, and begin. Ray sits next to me and helps me finish. We eat until all that's left is the juice. Just as I start drinking the green liquid, I get to thinking maybe there is such a thing as eating too many vegetables. My stomach twists and turns again.

"Ray! Ryan! What are you two doing?" Mom is standing in the doorway in her bathrobe that no longer wraps around her big belly. She turns the light on.

Just then, the front door opens and Dad walks in, coming home from work. When he comes into the kitchen and sees us sitting on the floor with empty pickle jars all over the floor and countertop, he asks the same exact question Mom did. "What are you two doing?"

"Well, somebody answer us, please," Mom says. Ray opens his mouth but instead of words coming out, he runs to the bathroom. Within seconds he is vomiting. I am not sure if hearing him makes me sick or if it would have happened anyway, but just when Mom looks at me searching for an answer, I stand up and get to the sink as fast as I can and start vomiting, too.

Mom sees what we've done and even though we did it for her, she doesn't seem too happy about it. She is fussing the whole time while helping me at the sink, rubbing my back and saying over and over, "I can't believe you two did this!" and "What were you thinking?"

Ray is back in the living room now, rubbing his stomach. He lies down on the sofa, looking like he's too weak to walk to his bedroom. I lie on the opposite side of the couch, putting my head on the armrest. Mom brings us cold ginger ales and sets them on the coffee table. She brings two paper bags and sets one in front of me, one in front of Ray.

My stomach begins to settle just a bit. And now I am sleepy because I haven't slept at all and I can see through the curtains that daylight is here. Ray and I go in and out of sleep as Mom and Dad clean up the mess we made.

Dad washes out the sink, the whole time shaking his head. Then, as he scrubs and scrubs, he starts laughing. Loud and full like he does when his friends are here and they are playing cards at the dining room table and tossing stories back and forth all night long. He laughs and laughs and then Mom starts laughing, too. Both of them stand in the kitchen looking at each other, then at the ice cube trays (that I didn't even get a chance to put in the freezer), then the empty jars, and they laugh and laugh.

Mom whispers, "I'd put them on punishment, but I have a feeling they're suffering enough." I see her sit down at the small table in the kitchen.

I close my eyes to the sound of Mom laughing and think, even though my plan failed, at least she is not stressed out right now. I wonder if my little sister is smiling, too.

5

What Summer Brings

Already July is here. It is early morning and I am in bed, sitting cross-legged with a book in my lap. I'm reading as much as I can so I can mark books off my Summer Reading Challenge bingo sheet. This is what I love about summertime. Summer brings extra hours, so I can stay with a book as long as I want. I don't have to leave it at the very best part because it is time to go to school or do homework. I take my time finishing the last chapter and run to show Mom that I finished the whole book. "I'm going to have to take you back to the library soon so you can get more books." Mom kisses me on my forehead.

I go into the kitchen, get my favorite bowl out of the cabinet and a spoon out of the drawer. There are two cereal options for breakfast. Neither of them is that great. They are both the fake brands from the bottom shelf at the grocery store. I grab an orange and pour cereal in the bowl and then add milk. The jug isn't too heavy because it's only half-full. This is because Ray drinks milk as much as he should drink water, always sneaking an extra glass when Mom and Dad are out of sight. But I see him, I know. I eat my cereal, peel my orange, and break it apart into four wedges.

We are having what Mom calls a lazy summer day. Nothing to do today, except pack for church camp. That's the other thing summer brings—camp is this weekend. Three whole days with KiKi and Amanda.

Ray comes into the kitchen and goes to the refrigerator. He takes the milk out of the fridge and drinks a gulp of milk straight from the carton. I give him the sternest look I can give him, the one Mom would definitely give. He shrugs and puts the milk back in the fridge, so of course now I don't want any milk ever again until we get a new gallon.

"Are you nervous about camp?" Ray asks. He sits next to me and takes one of my orange wedges without asking.

I pinch him. "Why would I be scared?"

"Because of the ghosts that come out at night," Ray says.

"Ray! Stop trying to scare your sister!" Mom shouts from the living room. No matter where she is, she always seems to know what we're up to. Her superpower is hearing even the tiniest sound from miles away.

Mom's warning to Ray about not scaring me is too late. Ray has already got my nerves going. Just the word *ghosts* has my heart beating fast, but I don't let Ray know that I'm afraid. "I don't care about ghosts. I'm excited to go to camp."

"Oh, good," Ray says. "Because they especially go after kids who are really scared, especially when kids hike the trails or go walking at night, and they haunt the cabins of the ones who are attending camp for the first time. Good thing you're not afraid."

I don't feel like finishing my orange. My stomach is spinning like the Carousel at Oaks Park.

Ray walks away with a creepy smile on his face.

I think he's just messing with me about ghosts haunting the camp. But how can I be sure?

"Ryan, when you're finished in the kitchen, let's get you ready for camp. You need to pack your bag." Mom is standing at the closet in the hallway pulling out my suitcase.

My stomach is still swirling.

Ray yells from his bedroom, "Don't forget bug spray. There's lots of big bugs that'll be crawling on you. Especially at night."

"Ray Hart! That's enough."

"What? I'm just trying to prepare her and tell her all she needs to know about camp."

"You're trying to scare her, and that's not okay."

I don't want to go anymore. Still, I won't admit it.

"I'm not afraid of ghosts or bugs or whatever else you tell me. Camp is going to be fun because Kiki and Amanda will be there and we're all in a cabin together. And even if something scary happens, we're best friends and best friends help each other, and—"

"You forgot about Red. Somebody named Red is coming, too," Ray tells me.

"No she's not, and how would you know? You've never even met Red."

"I've never met her, but I saw her name on the roster." Ray comes back into the kitchen holding his camp folder. He pulls out a sheet of paper. The top says *Room Assignments* and under Cabin Six—my cabin—the cabin that's supposed to be for me, KiKi, and Amanda—I see our names: Ryan Hart, KiKi Jones, Amanda Keaton.

And then, Red Harper.

"Mom, can I call Amanda?"

"Yes," Mom says. She gives me her cell phone, and

I call Amanda. I barely let her get out hello before I ask, "Is Red coming to church camp?"

"Yes. I invited her at the last minute, and Ms. Howard said I asked just in time. There was only one more spot left."

Amanda sounds happy about Red coming, like Red is not the person who was mean to me at her birthday party, like Red isn't competing with me to be Amanda's new best friend. Camp was supposed to be all about me, KiKi, and Amanda, back together again, a slumber party in the woods.

Amanda says, "Red is really nice once you get to know her. I thought it would be fun to have all my friends together. I asked Ms. Howard to put us all in the same cabin. We're going to have so much fun."

"Yeah," I mumble. "So much fun."

After I hang up the phone Ray says, "Told you," and goes back into his room to finish doing whatever he was doing.

Ray is right. Red is coming to camp. I'll have to spend three whole days with her. I go to my room with Mom and start packing, but really, I want to tell, Mom that I'll just stay here with her. Help out around the house since she's on bed rest and needs to take it easy. My stomach is swirling and swirling, and my heart is pounding and pounding.

If Ray is right about Red, maybe he is right about the bugs and the ghosts, too.

GETTING READY

6

I AM ALL FINISHED PACKING and spend the rest of the day reading. But this time, my mind can't keep still, can't focus on the words on the page. Instead, I keep thinking about camp and wondering what it's going to be like with Red there. I keep thinking how it's always been Amanda + KiKi + me. I don't want to add anyone else. Especially not Red.

Summer's breeze is seeping through my open bedroom window. The smell of freshly cut grass lingers in the air. The sun is fading away like the end of a song. Soon it will be time for dinner.

I hear the doorbell and then Grandma's voice

echoes through the house. Mom comes to my room, stands in the doorway, and says, "You want to help me and your grandma get the room ready for your baby sister?" Once my sister is old enough to sleep in a bed, Mom says she'll have a bed in my room, but until then, she'll be in Mom and Dad's room.

I put a bookmark in my book to hold my place and jump off the bed. We walk to Mom and Dad's bedroom. Dad has already started working on the room. Last week he painted one of the walls a soft gray color. He put the crib and changing table together. They are against the wall, next to each other. A mahogany chest with five drawers stands in the corner. It was a gift from Aunt Rose.

"What needs to be done?" Grandma asks.

"I thought we could put the sheets on the mattress in the crib and hang the wall art," Mom says. "And maybe one of us can finally sort through those clothes over there." She points to three canvas bags full to the brim. A woman from church dropped them off last week. Her daughter just turned one year old, so she doesn't need the baby clothes anymore. She told Mom everything in the bags was freshly washed and what Mom didn't want she could donate to Goodwill.

Grandma looks at the bags. "Well, I say, this little girl might have more clothes than all of us."

We laugh and then Grandma starts telling us what to do. Grandma is good at organizing people and things because she has had two children and helped to raise us grandchildren, so I think she knows what to do when it comes to getting ready for a baby. Grandma says, "Okay, Ryan sweetheart, you'll help me with the crib, and we'll hang the art. Your mom does not need to be on her feet." She gives Mom a stern look when she says this. "Tamia, you go on ahead and sit in the rocking chair and look through those bags. Fold what you want to keep and Ryan can put those in the drawers. Whatever you don't want, I'll drop off at Goodwill in the morning."

We begin.

I help Grandma with the fitted sheet on the crib. We tug and pull and get it on nice and snug. Mom holds up a piece of clothing, and if me and Grandma give it a thumbs-up, she refolds it and puts it in the keep pile. I take the clothes from the pile and put them in the drawers while Grandma puts the art on the wall, every now and then asking, "Is this straight?"

I guide her till she gets it just right.

"I feel like it's taking forever for the baby to come," I say.

"She'll be here soon enough," Grandma says.

"You always say that, Grandma. Soon enough."

Grandma chuckles. "Well, it's true. In most cases, if you can be patient, you'll have what you're waiting for soon enough."

"What about the flowers in your garden? When will they finally bloom?"

"Oh, those marigolds are taking their sweet ole time. They are just now sprouting, as they should be. But they'll be in full bloom soon enough."

Soon enough.

Soon enough.

Grandma always says *soon enough*.

Mom rubs her belly, and says, "Your grandma is right, Ryan. Love takes time to grow."

Once I've put away all the new baby clothes and the art is up and the crib is looking like it's ready to hold a sleeping baby, I step back and look at the whole room. I can't believe that just a few pieces of art, a crib, a dresser, and a painted wall have made this room look like a brand-new space. I think maybe I'll ask Dad to paint one of my walls, make this new (old) house look brighter.

We go into the kitchen to make dinner. I help Grandma, passing her what she needs because she can't find the right knife, spice, or plate. She doesn't let me do much more than that, even though I know my way around the kitchen, even though I am Mom's sous-chef and she lets me cut and slice and stir and taste test, not just pass her ingredients. We are making chicken tacos. Grandma stuffs them with lots of veggies that I've never seen go in tacos. She says we need to eat more vegetables.

"As long as it's not pickles," I say.

"Pickles? In tacos?"

"Never mind."

Grandma continues adding the veggies to the shells. Once I taste them, I realize they aren't so bad because they're disguised in sour cream and melted cheese and spicy salsa. Maybe I'll always stuff my tacos with veggies from now on.

At the dinner table Grandma says, "Ryan, we'll have to set a time for me to braid your hair before you leave for camp."

And just the word—*camp*—makes my stomach swirl and my heart pound again.

"If I braid it, you won't have to worry about doing it every day while you're away."

"Can I have beads on the ends?"

"Sure. I have some nice wooden beads we can use," Grandma says. "Ray, are you excited about camp?"

Ray shrugs. "I guess."

"You'll have to look out for your sister this year."

"I will," Ray says. He gets up to take his plate into the kitchen, and when he walks past my chair, he whispers, "I'll make sure the ghosts don't scare her."

And I can't even yell at him because no one heard him, so I'll look like I'm fussing at him for no reason. I get up to take my plate into the kitchen, too, and when I get away from Grandma and Mom, I whisper, "I'm not afraid of ghosts. So I'm not going to need you at all."

"Fine," Ray says. "I'll stay with my friends at camp and you stay with yours. We don't have to interact at all." He puts his plate in the dishwasher. "But I'm telling you, they're real and they love haunting the first years. You better be ready."

7

EVERY ROSE HAS ITS THORN

THE REST OF THE week goes by fast, and this means there's only one day left until I leave for camp. Sometimes I am excited to go, sometimes I am afraid. And not just afraid of the creepy bugs and spooky ghosts Ray keeps telling me about. I'm afraid that maybe Amanda invited Red because me and KiKi aren't her best friends anymore. Maybe the more time she spends with Red, the more she likes her and the less she likes us.

I think I will ask Grandma about this while she is braiding my hair. Grandma always gives good advice but especially when she is doing my hair. I'm not the only one who thinks this. Lots of women at church tell Grandma how much they miss her having her hair salon, but when I look at their hair, they look just fine. So I don't think it's just about hair. Usually, they say something like, "I really miss our conversations," or "Talking to you makes everything better," and I know what they mean. Grandma is easy to talk to. So now that she's here and sitting on the sofa waiting for me, I sit down on the floor—on top of a pillow for extra cushion—and get in position for her to do my hair. I don't waste any time filling her in on everything that's happening with me, KiKi, and Amanda.

"You're talking too fast. Slow down," Grandma says. "Who's Red? Have I met her?"

"No. Red is Amanda's new friend."

"*Amanda's* new friend, not yours?"

"Right. When Amanda moved she made new friends, and Red is one of them. She was mean to me at Amanda's birthday party and kept saying Amanda is her best friend, not mine."

"Well, why can't you both be Amanda's best friend?"

"Because Amanda already has me and KiKi. She doesn't need any more best friends. And besides, Red is mean." I tell Grandma how Red challenged everyone at Amanda's party to a contest.

"A contest?"

"To see who could hold their breath underwater the longest."

"When I won, she was still mean to me and teased me because my hair got all big and fluffy." I tell Grandma how I was the only Black girl at the pool party and how Red is white—and of course Grandma already knows that Amanda's mom is white and her dad is Black. "I was the only one looking different from everybody else."

"Oh my," Grandma says. "I'm really sorry that happened. Red sounds like a hard person to get along with."

"See—that's what I'm trying to tell you. I don't know why Amanda invited her. And I don't understand why Amanda thinks she needs a new friend."

62

I thought maybe Grandma already knew all of this, because sometimes it seems like Mom tells her everything.

Grandma stops braiding my hair and puts her hands on my shoulders, squeezes real tight like she is massaging love right into me. "You know, our hearts can hold love for a lot of people. You can have more than one best friend." Then she says, "I mean, you love KiKi *and* Amanda, right?"

"Yes."

Grandma is almost finished braiding my hair. She keeps talking about kindness and how there is always enough to give. "I think Amanda has love for all three of you and that's okay."

"I just wanted it to be me, KiKi, and Amanda having our first camp together."

Grandma says, "Well, I think you can figure out how to get along well enough not to make Amanda choose," Grandma says. "You never know what can grow between the two of you if you plant little seeds of kindness, of love. Might take a lot of nurturing and lots of patience, but things can change. Just may take some time."

I am thinking Grandma and I are done talking, but Grandma always has more to say, more to give.

"Sweetheart, I'm not saying you have to become friends with Red. You're not going to be friends with everyone and that's just fine. But I don't want you being unkind to her just to get her back for being nasty toward you. Instead, be a rose."

"A rose?"

"Yes. Be a rose. You know, every rose has its prickles—or what most of us call thorns."

"Yes—and they hurt when they prick your finger. Bad."

"Most people think those thorns are ugly, they think thorns represent flaws. But those thorns are there for a reason. To protect all that beauty," Grandma says. "Ryan, you have a lot of beauty to protect. You don't need to shrink to make anyone else feel important. Sometimes you're going to have to stand up for yourself—and others might think you're being a little prickly. But it's okay to let people know what you need and want. It's okay to tell Red to respect you. And if you need support, ask an adult at camp. Okay?"

"Yes, ma'am."

"You know, Red might be just as nervous about you as you are about her. Sometimes people are mean because they are jealous or intimidated or because they just haven't learned how to be nice. And you don't deserve that. So I want you to go to that camp and have fun with KiKi and Amanda, and if Red tries to pull you down, don't let her. You, KiKi, and Amanda have been friends for a really long time. You don't have anything to prove." Grandma gets out the wooden beads. The beads are different shades of brown and some are big, some are small. She puts a few on the ends of each braid. After she puts the last set of beads on, she gives me a handheld mirror so I can see myself. I shake my head so I can hear the beads knocking against each other.

"Thank you, Grandma."

"You're welcome."

We clean up, putting away the leftover beads, the comb, and hair oil. I put everything away in my hair basket and then Grandma reaches in her purse and pulls out two Werther's Originals hard candies. "One for now, one for later," she says.

I unwrap the candy and put it on the middle of my tongue.

I never get to stay up this late, but since Grandma was doing my hair I had special permission. Ray should be asleep, but once he saw I was staying up late he begged Mom to let him stay up, too. Grandma kisses my cheek and then calls for Ray and Mom so she can say good night to them both.

We say our goodbyes, and just as Mom is closing the door, Dad is opening it to leave for his night shift. He gives Ray and me the biggest hugs. As soon as Mom closes the door, she says, "All right. It's time for bed."

"But Mom!" Ray is protesting. "One more hour, please?" He's playing a video game and doesn't want to turn it off.

"Yeah, Mom, please? One more hour?" I beg. I've been reading as much as I can because I won't while I'm at camp. I just have one more X to add and I'll have bingo in one row.

"Thirty minutes," Mom says. "Then teeth brushed, prayers prayed, and in the bed."

I brush my teeth, say my prayers, and get into bed with my book and flashlight. I stay up longer than thirty minutes—and fall asleep reading.

ME + KIKI + AMANDA (+ RED)

SUMMER MORNINGS COME WITH a gentle breeze and don't feel like summer at all. But soon the sun will blaze its heat on us. It is seven o'clock, and Grandma picks us up to drive us to church so we can board the charter bus and head to the campgrounds. On our way to the church, we stop to get KiKi. She comes out with an overnight bag on her shoulder. It looks so heavy and is weighing her down, making her walk with a tilt like the Leaning Tower of Pisa. As soon as she gets in the car, I feel better about everything because having KiKi with me reminds me that I am not alone and that we can have fun doing anything, like how we are laughing while calling out license plates trying to beat Ray. We are teamed up, the two of us against him, and we only have a few more blocks to go before we are at church.

"Idaho!" we say at the same time. And then "California!" And we are tied with Ray, who saw two plates from Washington. We all have our faces pressed against the windows determined to break the tie.

"It's mighty early for you all to be so loud," Grandma says. "How about we all just calm down and listen to music for the rest of the ride." Grandma turns on her gospel music and we all get quiet. But then I see another Washington plate, and I can't help but to whisper it—loud. "Washington!"

KiKi raises her hands cheering silently and then whispers, "We beat you, Ray."

And Ray says, "Grandma said the game was over, so nope—we're still tied." Ray is not whispering, so I talk in my regular voice, too, telling him that we are not tied and that he is being a sore loser.

"All right, everybody, now I'd like some peace and quiet so I can hear my music." Grandma turns the knob up and for the next two blocks we listen to Fred Hammond, me and KiKi trying our best to keep our giggles in. KiKi points to a car with a Montana license plate. She mouths the word, and we laugh to ourselves because we are gaining even more points against Ray. We can't stop laughing. Grandma gives me a look from the rearview mirror, and I take a deep breath, try to hold it in.

When we pull up to the church, the first thing I see is the charter bus that is already being loaded with luggage on the bottom. Ms. Howard and Deacon LeRoy are the program directors. They are standing with the parent chaperones in a huddle with clipboards in their hands. They're married, and I don't think I've ever seen one without the other. Their daughter, Lizzy, is one of the teen counselors. She was a Rose Festival Princess last year, so I am glad I get a whole weekend with her because I can ask her all about it.

Olivia's mom, Ms. Lee, is here. She hardly ever lets Olivia go anywhere without her except school. I'm not surprised she's one of the chaperones. Olivia's cousin, Katie, is visiting from out of town, so she's here, too. She has braids like me, but no beads on the ends.

Most of the Sunday school crew is here, including Fast-Talking Bobby and Forgetful Gary. These nicknames started because of how they did their speeches this past Easter. No one has said my nickname to my face, but KiKi told me it's Runaway Ryan, because I bolted out of the sanctuary when I couldn't remember my poem. Ray sees Aiden and Logan (who are the ones who made up the nicknames), and they are waving at him and walking over to the car, waiting for us to get out.

We say our goodbyes to Grandma, and just as she drives off I hear Amanda calling my name. I turn around and see her running toward me. Her smile answers all of my questions. She wraps her arms around me, pulling KiKi in, too. The three of us hug and rock each other, and Amanda says, "We are going to have the best time."

Red is standing there watching us. I wave to her. "Hi, Red." I walk over to her. Amanda and KiKi follow.

Amanda says, "KiKi, this is Red. She's my neighbor."

"Hi, Red." KiKi is hesitant because I've told her everything about how Red treated me.

"Nice to meet you, KiKi," Red says. "Hi, Ryan." Red's voice is quiet and not as big as it was at Amanda's birthday. Even though Red is in jean shorts and a T-shirt just like us, she looks dressed up because her clothes are designer and I can tell what she's wearing is brand-new.

We board the bus, and I sit with KiKi, Amanda sits with Red. Both Amanda and I sit on the aisle so this way we are sitting next to each other, too. Once the bus starts rolling, it doesn't take long for the boys at the back of the bus to start freestyling. Ray is rapping to the rhythm of Logan's beat, who is tapping his pencil against the window and beatboxing. The whole bus is swaying and bobbing our heads.

KiKi goes into her backpack and pulls out a small plastic container. "Want some pretzels?" she asks.

"Thanks," I say. I pull out string cheese from my snack bag and we eat.

Just as we finish our snack, Ms. Howard calls out to everyone, "All right, listen up. Our returners already know this, but since we have new faces with us, I'm going to teach you all a song called 'The Name Game.' This way, we'll all get to know each other's names and have a little fun in the process." She is sitting on her knees, facing us, her back toward the driver of the bus. "Okay, so first I'm going to sing it doing my daughter's name, and I want you to listen for the rules. Got that? Those of you who already know how this goes can sing along."

Me, KiKi, and Amanda sing along because Ms. Howard taught this to us in Sunday school class a long time ago, back when Amanda still went to our church. Ms. Howard calls out "Lizzy!" and we sing as loud as we can:

Lizzy, Lizzy, bo-bizzy
Bonana-fanna, fo fizzy
Fee fi mo-izzy
Lizzy!

We all laugh because we know how silly we sound. Ms. Howard talks through it, slowly explaining the rules so the new people can catch on. Then she says,

"Okay, when I point to you, shout your name and then we'll all join in. Ready?" Ms. Howard points to Gary. We do Gary first, then Ray, then Katie. We all sing:

Katie!
Katie, Katie, bo-batie
Bonana-fanna fo-fatie
Fee fi mo-matie, Katie!

A few of the new people aren't singing along, and Red looks terrified when it becomes her turn. She does shout her name out, but after that, she doesn't sing along. Her face turns the color of her name and she just sits there. I did not expect Red to be so mild. She is nothing like the girl I met at Amanda's pool party. I guess now she knows it's not so easy to just fit in when you're the new girl. I nudge Amanda, point out that Red is not singing. Amanda takes her hand, sings it louder, and eggs her on to join in. Red tries and she fumbles over the rhymes a little, but then she gets it, and once we're at Amanda, she has it down and is singing and laughing with the rest of us.

NEVER LETTING GO

9

WE RIDE THE BUS for an hour and a half before we are at the campgrounds. The bus stops, and the driver gets off and starts unloading our bags. Deacon LeRoy helps him. Ms. Howard says, "Please wait to exit the bus until your name is called. Each room has a youth counselor assigned to it. I will say their name and then call out the cabinmates. When you exit the bus, please stand with your youth counselor."

Our counselors are all in college. Some of them are back for the summer and this is their job. Ms. Howard reads off our room assignments, and we walk to our cabins with our youth counselor. Me, KiKi, Amanda, and Red are with Lizzy, which I love because she is the only one I really know.

When we get to our room, Lizzy says, "Okay, you four are in there, and my room is here." The rooms are tiny, ours with two bunk beds so all four of us can sleep in one room. Her room has one bunk bed, and I'm sure she'll just sleep on the bottom.

Even though I am with KiKi and Amanda and so far Red hasn't said too much to bother me, I am starting to miss home. I wonder what Mom is doing and if my little sister is tossing and turning in her belly. Wonder if they miss me yet.

Lizzy asks us to come sit in the common area, where the sofas and coffee table are. "We need to choose a cabin captain," Lizzy says. "The captain is responsible for keeping the group together, making sure you all show up for meals, Bible study, and campfire prayer circle on time. The captain will also direct the theater skit that each cabin will perform at the end of the weekend."

"A skit? About what?" KiKi asks.

"You'll get more info about that later today. Right now, we just need to choose who the captain will be. Which one of you is a leader?"

I think about what Dad and Mom always tell me about being who they named me to be. I raise my hand. "What does the cabin captain have to do again?" I know the answer. I just need to hear it one more time.

Lizzy repeats the responsibilities.

"I think Ryan would be good at that," Amanda says.

"Me too." KiKi leans back on the sofa and then says, "And I can be her assistant." She laughs and I laugh and Amanda does too, but Red isn't laughing or smiling at all.

Lizzy asks me, "Do you want to do it, Ryan?"

"Yes," I say.

"Great." Lizzy writes my name on the top of a sheet of paper on her clipboard. Then she says, "And, KiKi, you can help her out if she needs it." The last thing Lizzy tells us is, "You have about thirty minutes to get settled and then we have an important meeting in the dining hall."

KiKi says, "Let's go for a walk. I want to see what's around here."

We all stand and head out of the cabin.

Lizzy calls to us, "Dining hall in thirty minutes. Be on time."

"Okay," we say.

The campus is surrounded by trees watching over us. We walk around the campgrounds, following the signs to find our way. The whole time we walk, I am swatting at flies and mosquitoes and I remember what Ray said about all the bugs. He is right. I will put my bug spray on as soon as I get back to my room. We follow the signs to the main lodge and go inside. There's a fireplace and lots of comfy sofas and chairs to sit on. There are bookshelves with board games, coloring books, and puzzles, and the windows are so big, so long, they let in all the sky's light. Behind the lodge, there's a pond where ducks are swimming.

I think we should come back and feed them, but then I see a sign that says Please Don't Feed the Ducks.

The four of us are standing at the window watching the ducks float on the water. One of them is so still, it doesn't look real. Katie comes over to us and says, "We need one more player in order to start this game. Anyone want to play?" She points to one of the tables where Bobby and Gary are setting up a board game.

Red smiles. "That's one of my favorites. I'll play." She walks over to the table and joins them.

"Let's go outside and see what Olivia is doing," I say. KiKi and Amanda walk with me to the wraparound porch, where Olivia is with a girl named Brianna. They are standing at the far left end of the porch playing Slide, the hand-clapping game. They get to seven before Olivia messes up. "Ugh! One more time," she says. They go again and this time they only get to four.

I am laughing because Olivia is so frustrated. I say, "Let's play Sweet, Sweet Baby."

"Oh, yeah, that way we can all play," Olivia says. She steps back from Brianna, making room for me, KiKi, and Amanda to join. We form a circle and get our arms and hands into position.

KiKi calls out, "Ready?" and we start the song:

Down down baby, down down the roller coaster,
Sweet, sweet baby, I'll never let you go,

Shimmy, shimmy cocoa pops,
Shimmy, shimmy pow!
Shimmy, shimmy cocoa pops,
Shimmy, shimmy pow!

And then my favorite part:

Let's get the rhythm of the head . . .
Let's get the rhythm of the hands . . .
Let's get the rhythm of the feet . . .

Our claps echo under the clouds. It is so quiet out here in the woods, so peaceful that I wonder if we are being too loud, but then I think maybe the trees and the bushes and all the nature surrounding us like the company, like having our voices fill up the empty spaces.

When we get to the end, we sing the last part backward. And when it's all over, we do it again. Once we are finished with our hand-clapping game, Amanda says, "Want to jump rope?"

"I don't think we have time," I say. I notice a line of campmates walking toward the dining hall. "We can't be late to the dining hall." I go into the game room and call for Red and everyone else who is still playing games or sitting on the sofas talking.

We all walk to the dining hall, the gravel crunching under our feet. I am in the middle of KiKi and Amanda, and it is just how it is supposed to be. The hand-clapping song is stuck in my head. I sing it over and over. *Sweet, sweet baby, I'll never let you go.*

Love Your Neighbor as Yourself

10

When we get to the dining hall, there are snacks set out for us and packets are sitting in the middle of the round tables—enough for each person. I get an apple, KiKi gets an orange, Red gets a bag of mini pretzels, Amanda doesn't want anything. While we wait for Ms. Howard to get started, I take one of the packets from the stack and look through it. We have a Bible story to read and discussion questions on the second page.

"All right, everyone, let me explain our theater project. Please sit with your cabinmates," Ms. Howard says. Ms. Lee is next to her, looking out at us, making sure we are following directions. "Each cabin will be pulling a piece of paper out of this bag. You will have a scripture and a phrase on that paper. You are to create a short skit acting out the scripture for a special performance. You will have time today and tomorrow with your youth counselor to talk about the scripture and practice."

The youth counselors pass the bag around, and we are the second group to choose. Amanda digs into the bag, and I can tell she is mixing up the slips of paper before she pulls one out. She opens it and says, "The Good Samaritan, Luke 10:25–37." She passes the paper, and when KiKi gets it, she reads it and says, "Our phrase is 'Love your neighbor as yourself.'"

We are dismissed to go with our cabinmates to any part of the campus so we can have private time to read the scripture and begin our discussion. Lizzy takes my group to the back porch of the dining hall, and we sit on the steps. Lizzy says, "Let's each take a turn reading from the handout out loud and then we can discuss. Who would like to read first?"

None of us raise our hands, so I say, "I'll go first," because I am the cabin captain.

After we read the scripture, Lizzy asks us questions to make sure we understand the story. "Okay, let's discuss. What happened in this parable?" She calls on Red even though Red doesn't have her hand up.

"Oh, um, there was a man traveling and on the way he was attacked by really bad guys who took his clothes and left him beat up on the side of the road."

I add, "And then a priest walked by, but instead of helping the man, he crossed to the other side of the road and just left him there."

Amanda says, "Another person came by and just ignored him too, but the third man—the good Samaritan—was kind and took care of him."

Lizzy wipes sweat from her forehead and scoots over to get more into the shade. She puts on her sunglasses. "Does anyone remember how the Good Samaritan helped?"

I blurt out, "He bandaged the man's wounds, took him to an inn, and told the innkeeper to take good care of him and let the man have whatever he needs. He even paid for it all."

Lizzy says, "And this was a big deal because the two men came from different places and it was against social norms for them to interact. One of the lessons this parable teaches us is that *everyone* is our neighbor—no matter where they come from, no matter their religion, the color of their skin, or how much money they have." Lizzy stands and turns her back to the sun. She leans against the banister and says, "So Jesus said, 'Go and do the same,' and I want us to think about what this means in our everyday lives."

Lizzy gives us a moment to think and then she says, "You don't have to answer this out loud, but I want you to ask yourself these questions: Who is your neighbor? How can you show kindness even to people who are different from you?"

Lizzy pauses for a long time, giving space for us to think before she moves on to the next thing. "In your folder, you'll find blank sheets of paper. Write down three ways you will love your neighbor as yourself, or in other words, three ways you will practice kindness."

I think about the homeless people I've seen down-town when I go with Mom to Saturday Market. I want to give them good food, something I make especially for them. I write that down. For my second thing, I write down that I will be the best big sister in the world, and before I get my third answer down, Lizzy says, "Okay, let's move on to getting our performance together."

I slide my paper back in the folder. I'll come up with a third kindness later.

We spend the rest of our morning session plotting out our skit. Lizzy says, "I'm going to let you all take the lead." She looks at me when she says this.

I say to the group, "First, we need to figure out who will play each role."

"I want to be the priest who passes by," Red says. *Of course she wants to play a mean person,* I think.

KiKi says, "Hold on—Ryan gets to choose because she is our cabin captain and is the director of our skit."

I think maybe I should make Red be the Good

Samaritan so she can practice being nice for once. And then I think maybe we can play rock-paper-scissors and decide that way. That always works for me and Ray.

I realize I haven't said anything yet and we've got to get started. I think of an even better idea than rock-paper-scissors. "Let's pull names," I say. That way I am deciding but in the most fair way. I take out a sheet of blank paper, and I rip it into four pieces. I use Lizzy's Sharpie to write the main characters down and then fold each piece of paper.

"Great idea, Ryan." Lizzy takes the four slips of paper and mixes them up in her hands. "Okay, who's picking first?"

"My assistant, KiKi," I say.

KiKi smiles and closes her eyes and takes one of the folded papers out of Lizzy's hand. "I'm the priest!" she shouts. She looks happy about it, and I can't tell if she really wanted that role or if she's gloating that she got what Red wanted.

Amanda chooses next. She closes her eyes and

accidentally picks up two pieces of paper. She puts one back and opens the other. "I'm the Levite—the second man who passes by."

Maybe my plan is working. Red will have to be the Good Samaritan.

I can see that other groups have been dismissed from their morning sessions. Laughter fills the campgrounds, and I see groups heading to the game room and others to the main lodge. I want Red to hurry up and choose so we can join the others and play before lunch. "Your turn, Red," I say.

Red pulls her piece of paper. When she unfolds it, she says, "I'm the man on the side of the road." She puts the thin paper in the pocket of her jean shorts.

"Ryan, that means you're the Good Samaritan," Lizzy says. She gives me the last piece of paper.

Wait, what? I'm the one who's going to have to rescue Red? I'm the one who has to pretend to go out of my way to be kind to her?

So much for my plan.

11

BUGS AND GHOSTS

WE END THE DAY at the fire pit with a sing-along and prayer. When we started the campfire, the sun was just setting, but now the sun is gone and the stars look like scattered pearls across the sky. "This will be our nightly ritual," Ms. Lee says. After we sing and pray, we are dismissed back to our cabins. The trees are only shadows now against the dark sky. The pond has disappeared against the blackness, and I can't see the rolling hills of trees anymore, but I can feel them. I know that they are looming over us, and for some reason, now that it's nighttime, those trees feel creepy and are not comforting at all. I keep close to

KiKi and Amanda, walking in the middle of them, for extra security.

I wish the walk wasn't so far from our cabin. And I wish Ray, Aiden, and Logan would stop making random noises as we walk. One of them keeps clicking his tongue like a snake, and someone else keeps hooting like an owl. How did they get so good at sounding like animals? All of their noises mixed with the very real sound from the chorus of crickets is making me want to run back to the cabin and stay inside until it's daylight.

The whole way back to the cabin, KiKi is complaining about her itching arm. Her right arm has welts because she's been bitten by mosquitoes and won't stop scratching the bites. I don't say, *I told you so*, but I absolutely did tell her to spray her arms and legs with my bug spray before we left for the campfire, and I absolutely did tell her *who cares if it smells like medicine* when she told me she didn't want to walk around smelling like an old person with achy joints.

"Stop scratching," Lizzy says. "I know it's hard not to scratch, but you're going to make it worse."

"Nothing can be worse than this," KiKi says.

And just when she says this, a figure jumps out of the woods making an eerie sound. We all start running. Except for Lizzy. Lizzy is calm and cool, and she is laughing, calling out, "I don't who that was, but it's bedtime in ten minutes, so I hope you're making your way back to the cabins."

How does she know it's not a ghost? A real ghost who is coming after us because all of us—me, KiKi, Amanda, and Red—are first-timers.

"Ladies, are we okay?" Lizzy asks. She is just a little out of breath because she had to run to catch up with us. "I'm sure it's just some of the boys being silly."

We are all breathing hard and walking so fast, the dust is kicking up and the pebbles crackle under our feet like the logs in the campfire flames. When we first started walking back to the cabins, I was between KiKi and Amanda, but now that we've been running, we are in a different order. I am beside Lizzy and Red. KiKi and Amanda are in front of us. The crickets are chirping, and I can hear the creek water spilling on itself even though I can't see it. And this makes me even more terrified because I know there are things here that I can't see, so that means there really could be ghosts following us. I feel something take my hand and I jump and pull away, but then I realize it's Red. She's taken my hand and is holding on tight. I take Lizzy's hand, and we walk back to the cabin in total silence because we all have agreed that maybe if we're quiet the ghosts won't hear us, won't bother us.

Since it's so quiet, I can hear everything that's happening. I hear giggling from the bushes, and I know that ghosts don't giggle. I also know the sound of my brother's laugh, how when he's trying to hold it in, he chuckles in a way that sounds like air oozing out of a balloon, then getting sucked in again.

"Ray? Ray, I know that's you. Stop trying to scare us!" I yell out into the darkness. There are footsteps

94

running and a burst of laughter from different voices. I'm pretty sure it's Ray, Aiden, and Logan.

When we get back to the cabin, Lizzy says, "I'll be right back. I'm going to check in with the youth counselor over at Cabin Four." Cabin Four is Ray's cabin. I'm glad Lizzy is going to tell them to leave us alone.

We take turns going in and out of the bathroom to brush our teeth and get ready for bed. Once everyone is ready, we go into the bedroom and get into the bunk beds. Me and Red on the top bunks. KiKi under me, Amanda under Red. We are all quiet. Just when I figure they've fallen asleep, Red says, "Ryan, do you really think it was your brother and his friends who scared us?"

"I'm sure of it."

It is quiet again, and then after a while, Red says, "I know how we can get them back." I hear her moving and then the light comes on. She climbs down the ladder of the bunk bed and goes into her suitcase. "Tomorrow night after the fireside sing-along, we

95

can scare them with these." Red pulls a too-real-looking plastic rat out of her bag and holds it up in her right hand. In her left hand, she has a snake. "I have a bunch of these in my bag."

"You have more of those in your suitcase?"

"Yeah, the more the better. One wouldn't scare anybody."

I know they're not real, but I still hide in my sleeping bag. I do not want to see that at all. KiKi shrieks, "Put them away. I'm going to have nightmares."

Amanda asks, "Why do you even have those? What did you plan on doing with them?"

Red puts them back in her suitcase, zips them in, and climbs into her bunk. "I thought maybe they'd come in handy. Just in case I wanted to play a prank on someone." She turns the light off.

I can't help but wonder if Red was planning to prank me. Or maybe me and KiKi. This whole time she's had those in her suitcase just waiting for the perfect moment to use them.

Red says, "Those boys are going to be soooo scared tomorrow."

We all laugh, but as quiet as we can, making sure we don't make too much noise and alarm Lizzy. Knowing that we will get Ray, Aiden, and Logan back for messing with us makes me less afraid, and I fall asleep imagining how funny it's going to be.

12

REVENGE

The **NEXT MORNING,** I wake up forgetting where I am. Just for a moment, I think I will open my eyes and see my room and hear Mom's slippers dragging across the hallway floor, coming to wake me up when I am already up. And when I remember where I am, I feel sad. Just a little. Not enough to cry or want to go home, but I do want to call Mom, hear her voice. I do want to feel Dad's arms wrapped around me, squeezing me like a too-tight coat. I want to put my hands on Mom's belly and feel my baby sister kick and move and wave hello.

I get out of bed, get dressed, and wait for the

others so we can go to the dining hall for breakfast.

On our way over, Red says, "Let's not ask the boys any questions about last night. We have to play it cool, like it's no big deal that they scared us."

I agree even though deep down, I want Ray to know that I am telling Mom and Dad how he treated me, that he did not protect me like big brothers are supposed to do.

When we walk into the dining hall, Ray and his friends immediately start acting overly nice to us.

"Do you have a place to sit?" Aiden asks. "Come over here with us."

And Logan says, "There's a waffle maker over there. I bet you make good waffles, Ryan."

"I sure do. Too bad I won't be making one for you. Or you either, Ray!" I roll my eyes, and Amanda nudges me because I am definitely not playing along with the whole just-act-normal agreement.

Just as breakfast is ending, Ms. Howard gets up and stands at the front of the room to make announcements before she sends us out to practice our skits. The first few announcements are reminders about respecting the space. "I know your mommas and daddies don't let you leave garbage around the house, so we aren't going to do that here. Please be sure to pick up after yourselves and throw away candy wrappers, napkins, soda cans . . . clean up what you mess up. Amen?"

We don't respond.

"I said amen! Are you all in agreement with me?"

"Yes," we say in unison, with a few *amens* sprinkled in the crowd.

We spend the rest of the day rehearsing for our performances. After dinner, it's showtime. I am not the best at performing in front of a lot of people, so I am glad that even though I have an important role, I don't have that many lines to remember. We practice and practice, and I almost start laughing at how good KiKi is at walking past Red, giving her the most disgusted look as she passes her on the side of the road. I think KiKi is enjoying having an excuse to be cruel to Red.

We are the fourth group to go. So far, of the groups who've performed, Ray's group was the best. They did the story of David and Goliath, and Ray did rap interludes to narrate the story.

KiKi, Amanda, Red, and I take our places, and Lizzy begins narrating. Everything is going as we practiced. KiKi and Amanda are perfect at walking past Red and ignoring her. When I come out, I do my part, pretending to nurse Red's wounds and walking her to the inn down the road. When we get to KiKi, who is now acting as the innkeeper, she says, "Hello, how may I help you?"

"One room please," I say. "Please take good care of my neighbor. If there's anything she needs, give it to her." I hand fake money that I drew to Amanda and then I say, "And if this isn't enough, I'll pay you more on my way back through town."

Red limps away offstage as if she is going to a room. I wave and walk the opposite way, as if I am leaving and going to my next destination. Then Lizzy starts narrating again. She asks the audience, "Three people notice the man on the side of the road. Which one showed love to their neighbor?"

Everyone in the room shouts in unison, "Number three."

Then me, KiKi, Amanda, and Red all stand at the front of the stage and say, "Go and do the same!"

We take our bow to a room full of applause. I remembered my lines, did everything as we practiced, and I had more fun than I thought I would, but I'm glad it's over.

After the performances, we end the evening at the fire pit.

We are waiting for Deacon LeRoy to sing the songs when Red says, "Amanda, don't you have to go the restroom?"

Amanda says, "No," looking confused.

"Um, well, I do, and I need you to come with me,"

Red says. "We'll be back." She grabs Amanda's arm and walks toward the cabins, giving me and KiKi a look, like she can't say where she's going out loud but we should already know.

KiKi whispers, "I think they're going to set up the boys' room."

Just the thought of it makes me want to laugh. I can't wait to hear the boys screaming out of fear. We cover for Amanda and Red, saying they needed to use the restroom since there aren't any out here.

Deacon LeRoy leads us in songs, and during the last one, KiKi's voice bellows out louder than anyone's. Ms. Howard ends the night with a prayer. Then she says, "And before we dismiss, let me make one thing clear." Ms. Howard's voice changes. It makes me sit up straight. "It's come to my attention that there are pranks being played at night."

When she says this, KiKi pinches the side of my leg and whispers, "Does she know about our plan?"

"There's no way she could know," I whisper.

Ms. Howard continues. "Let me remind you that

you all are expected to respect each other. If you haven't seen it yet, there's a game room on campus, equipped with board games, cards to play games, video games . . . there's all kinds of games. So I don't want to see any pranks being played. The only things being played ought to be in that game room. Amen?"

We all say, "Amen," loud and clear so she really hears us, believes us. Even though I know so many of us have no intention of keeping our word.

On our way back to the cabin, KiKi and I trail behind the group just a bit, our flashlights brightening the path. KiKi talks real low. "I have my phone with me, and I'm going to get video of the boys screaming and yelling."

I laugh. "They have no idea what's about to happen."

We catch up with Lizzy and Olivia, Bobby and Gary. The whole time, I have flutters in my belly like fireflies wanting to get loose.

Ray, Aiden, and Logan are just ahead of us. We are back up the hill at the cul-de-sac where the cabins are. Ray and his friends aren't even at their door yet when we hear a loud scream from their cabin.

If Ray, Aiden, and Logan are with their youth counselor outside, who's in their cabin?

The door bursts open, and Deacon LeRoy comes running out. "Oh, Lord. Oh my Lord." He is holding his chest, and his face is drenched in sweat.

Lizzy rushes up to him. "Dad, are you okay? Are you okay?"

What's going on? Are you okay?"

"Snakes! Snakes are everywhere in there. Big ole snakes!"

Those fireflies in my belly are fluttering even stronger.

What was Deacon LeRoy doing in their room?

Deacon LeRoy runs down the steps and even though there's a porch light on, he must not see that there's a third step. He misses it and his body leaps forward, and he falls into the dirt.

Ms. Howard rushes over to him. Ms. Lee asks for two of the youth counselors to help search the cabin and capture the snakes. Lizzy takes Deacon LeRoy to our cabin so he can sit for a moment and gather himself.

I look at Amanda and whisper, "You two put all of them out?"

"We rigged their front door so when it opened all the snakes would fall down."

"Amanda!"

"It was Red's idea."

KiKi talks but barely moves her lips. "And what about the rats?"

"In their beds, hidden in their sleeping bags."

"We have to say something," I tell them.

"We? Red and Amanda did it, not us," KiKi says. "But we knew they were going to. We planned it with them."

KiKi rolls her eyes. She nudges Amanda. "You have to say something."

Amanda looks like she's seen a ghost. A real live one. She is standing there with her mouth wide open. And if I couldn't hear how hard she is breathing, I'd think she was a statue.

I can tell that even the youth counselors are scared to go in Ray's cabin with Ms. Howard. They are walking slow and looking at the ground, making sure none of the snakes are there. Just as they get to the door, I say, "Wait. It's—it's not real. The snakes are not real." I walk toward Ray's cabin.

KiKi and Amanda follow me. KiKi says, "And there are fake rats in there, too."

Amanda steps onto the creaky porch. "I can show you." She goes inside and comes out with an armful of plastic snakes and rats.

"Girls, go into your cabin right now." Ms. Howard is not yelling, and I really wish she would. This calm, cold voice is not helping my fluttering stomach.

We file into our cabin. Deacon LeRoy is sitting on the sofa taking deep breaths, still recovering.

"Show him," Ms. Howard says.

Amanda holds out her arms. "Deacon LeRoy, we're sorry. We were just trying to play a prank on the boys because they were messing with us last night."

Deacon LeRoy looks at Amanda's arms and reaches out to touch them. "Well, I say! You had this old man fooled. I about had a heart attack."

"And that's nothing to play with!" Ms. Howard says. "Almost scared this man to death." Ms. Howard sits next to Deacon LeRoy. "Lizzy, what kind of youth counselor are you if you can't even—"

"It's not her fault," I say. "I'm cabin captain and I could have stopped us, but I didn't. We really, really are sorry."

Ms. Howard looks at Red, who is just standing against the wall, not saying a word. "You want to add anything, young lady?"

"I-I didn't know anything about it," Red says.

"Liar!" I yell.

Ms. Howard looks at me. "We're not going to have name calling added on to what's already been a disrespectful night."

"Ryan really wanted to get back at her brother."

"But, Ms. Howard, we all planned it," I say. KiKi nods. "Yeah, I knew it was happening, too."

"Red is the one who brought these here. I went with her to place them in Ray's cabin," Amanda says.

"Is this true, Red?" Ms. Howard asks.

"No, I swear. I don't know anything about this." I don't mean to yell, but I can't help it. "Red, that's not true. You can't just put the blame on us. This was all your idea, and we went along with it."

"We'll deal with this in the morning. I will definitely be calling all of your parents tomorrow," Ms. Howard says. "You all need to go to bed." She looks at her husband. "You okay?" She touches his hand and rubs his head.

"Lord, Lord. I'm okay, I'm okay." Deacon LeRoy stands and dusts off the dirt from his pants. He walks out with Ms. Howard.

"Bye, Dad," Lizzy says. She is shaking her head like she is in disbelief, or disappointed at us. Maybe both.

I offer another apology, calling out, "We're really sorry," as they walk down the steps of the porch, Deacon LeRoy limping all the way.

Lizzy closes the door and doesn't even ask us any questions. She just says, "Good night," and turns the lights out.

We lay in the dark and I can't sleep, can't stop thinking about how Red blamed it all on us, how I've tried to be kind to her and still she finds a way to be mean. Grandma's words always come back to me just when I need them. I am a rose and I have to protect my beauty, stand up for myself, even it means being prickly.

I'm not sure who's sleeping and who's awake. Maybe no one will hear me say this, but I speak anyway. "Red, that wasn't right what you did tonight. You know the truth, and you need to tell Ms. Howard what happened."

I hear someone shift and move in their bunk. Someone is awake. I think we all are.

I keep my eyes closed when I open my mouth to say, "You might be Amanda's friend, but if you don't tell the truth tomorrow, you're not mine."

13

JOY UNSPEAKABLE

LIKE A LONG MORNING yawn, the sun is stretching and rising and starting the day. It's the third day of camp. Tomorrow morning we'll be going home. I've been awake for a while because I can't sleep. I can't stop thinking about how much trouble we're going to be in today and how once we get home, we'll be in even more trouble.

Once we're all awake and dressed, we go to the dining hall for breakfast. Lizzy is walking with us, but she doesn't say much. Just *good morning* and that's it. None of us are talkative, especially not to Red. Even Amanda is giving her the silent treatment.

When we're finished eating, Ms. Howard comes to our table and says, "You all come with me." She takes us back to our cabin and takes out her cell phone. "KiKi, you come inside with me first. The rest of you stay out here on the porch."

Amanda and I sit next to each other. Still no talking. Red is sitting alone on the bottom step. I know KiKi is going to be on punishment. And as soon as she hangs up from her mom, her mom will call mine. They tell each other everything, especially when it comes to me and KiKi. So, by the time I call Mom, she might already know.

KiKi comes out wiping tears. She says, "Amanda, Ms. Howard said you're next."

"What's your punishment?" I ask.

KiKi says, "No electronics for a week."

That's not so bad. At least we'll still get to see each other. Well, depending on what my punishment is.

Amanda comes out and I know I am next, so I stand up before she tells me. She is not crying, but she looks sad. "Are you grounded?" I ask.

"My mom said she'll have to think about my punishment." Amanda sits next to KiKi, and I go inside the cabin.

Ms. Howard already has my mom on the phone when I walk in the room. She is doing more nodding and listening than talking and then she says, "Oh, well, I'm glad you've already talked with Ms. Jones . . . yes, I know KiKi and Ryan are good friends. I usually don't have any problems out of them . . . Yes, yes, she's right here." Ms. Howard hands me the phone.

"Mom?"

"I am very disappointed in you, Ryan."

"I'm sorry."

"Did you apologize to Deacon LeRoy?"

"Yes."

"You better be glad no one was hurt."

With Mom on bed rest, I'm supposed to be on my best behavior, but she sounds really, really, upset right now. "Ryan, I just— What were you thinking?"

"I just wanted to get Ray back because he was scaring us, and we—"

"Don't make excuses. You had a choice to make, and you made the wrong decision. I'll deal with Ray, too, but right now I'm talking with you. What do I always tell you? Be the leader we've raised you to be. You know better."

"But Red is the one who brought them here and I just—"

"Ryan Hart." Whenever Mom says my first and last name I know she means business. "Deacon LeRoy could've hurt himself—"

"I'm sorry."

"I sure hope it was worth it. Enjoy this last day with KiKi and Amanda, because you are not going to be doing anything with any of your friends for a week."

I don't cry or say anything else. At least I know Ray is going to get in some kind of trouble, too. Mom keeps on with her lecture. "And I expect you to be your best self for the rest of camp. I better not get another phone call about you. Do you understand me?"

"Yes."

"Give the phone back to Ms. Howard, please,"

Mom says. "And Ryan?"

"Yes?"

"I love you, okay?"

"Love you, too." I hand the phone back to Ms. Howard and go outside.

Red is next, and she's inside the longest. I can hear Ms. Howard fussing at her, and I don't even think she's called her mom yet. Lizzy comes to get me, KiKi, and Amanda. "We're having community-building activities in the gym," she says.

When we get to the gym, Ms. Lee tells us, "We are one community, and it is important to learn how to love and respect each other. This afternoon we will be playing several fun games to help us grow closer."

Most times when adults call something fun it is not fun at all, so I am not looking forward to these games. Red and Ms. Howard come in just as Ms. Lee gives the instructions. She tells us to get into a huddle and says, "Pretend we are on the first floor of an elevator. We have to make it to the twelfth floor. The way we get there is by one person calling out a number at a time in numerical order. If two voices shout out a number, we'll have to go all the way back to the first floor and start over. Any questions?"

No one has a question.

Counting to twelve seems so easy, but not with thirty kids who all want a turn.

We're on our third try. I start this time. "One," I shout.

KiKi says, "Two."

Aiden says, "Three."

A boy named Rodney says, "Four."

And on and on we go till Ray says, "Ten."

We have never made it this high. Two more floors and we'll be at the top.

It is quiet and then finally, the number eleven is blurted out. By two people.

We all groan because this means we have to start

116

all over again. I think about it and wonder how we can get a system going so each person knows when to go. I start off again. "One," I say. And this time, I make eye contact with Olivia. I nod toward her, like I am passing her the next number.

Olivia nods. *"Two."*

She looks at Ray and nods at him. He says, "Three."

And it keeps on going till we are at the number eleven. And finally, Amanda says, "Twelve!" and we all cheer.

The games keep coming, and right before it's time to break for dinner, our youth counselors lead us in a reflection. "How were you able to win the games we played today?" Lizzy asks.

Hands go up, and Lizzy calls on Brianna. "We had to listen to each other," she says.

And Bobby says, "We needed to be patient sometimes and wait our turn."

Ms. Lee asks, "Would anyone like to share what you learned about yourself?"

I raise my hand and say, "I learned that I'm a good problem solver."

Ms. Howard says, "Very good, all of you." She tells us that we need to remember how to be good listeners, how to be patient, and how to solve problems in our everyday lives, not just when we're playing games. She tells us she's proud of us for not giving up even when it was frustrating. "This is our community. We have to find ways to keep our community strong, and we have to find ways to work with each other."

Even though this whole mess happened with Red and the boys, I am kind of sad to be leaving camp tomorrow. Tonight, at the evening campfire, before the singing starts, Ray, Aiden, and Logan walk over to us, and Logan says, "Hey, we're sorry for scaring you the other night. It was just meant to be a joke. Sorry if we really made you afraid."

"We weren't *that* afraid," KiKi says. And then she

whispers, "But you all should be thankful Deacon LeRoy was doing his room check, because if a man like him was that scared of something fake, you three probably would've run all the way back to Portland."

And we start laughing.

Deacon LeRoy is sitting on a log next to Ms. Howard. "We're going to start tonight's singing with one of my favorite songs," he says. "It's an old song that you young folk might not know, but I'm going to teach it to you. It's a song about prayer and consecration," he tells us. "It's called 'I Fall Down on My Knees.'"

Bobby whispers, "Uh, literally. Like he literally fell down on his knees."

There are giggles behind me, and I am trying so hard not to laugh.

Then, Deacon LeRoy says, "I guess I could have written the song myself, huh?"

And I just can't hold it in. I burst into laughter. The laughter is contagious, and it is spreading and spreading. Even the youth counselors are laughing, even Lizzy. KiKi and Amanda are bent over holding their stomachs. And Red lets out the biggest snort I've ever heard, and that just makes us all laugh harder. Except Ms. Howard. She isn't laughing at all—but it looks like she wants to. I take deep breaths to calm down because this is the kind of laugh that might not ever stop.

I look up at the sky. It is black and massive, and I imagine that even the stars are tickled by what they see in us. They are twinkling, twinkling, catching our joy.

MAKING S'MORES

14

AFTER PRAYER, MS. HOWARD tells us that we have a special treat since it's our last night. The youth counselors have prepared all the fixings for making s'mores and placed them out on the wooden picnic table. The marshmallows look like miniature clouds in a bowl, and the chocolate bars are stacked like bricks. There are trays of graham crackers and long, thin wooden sticks on the table, too.

She calls on Olivia's cabin to go to the table first.

Ray points to all the other goodies on the table. There's a container of peanut butter, Oreos, a bowl of fruit, and other snacks. "What's all that for?" Ray asks.

"In case you want to mix it up," I say. "I think I'm going to make peanut butter s'mores: spread peanut butter on my graham crackers first, then add the chocolate and marshmallow."

"Do you always have to experiment?" Ray asks.

"I'm just going to roast marshmallows. Keep it simple."

"Simple as in bland," I say.

"Peanut butter and chocolate sounds amazing," Amanda says. "Ryan, I'm going to do that, too."

Red is listening in and watching us. She doesn't say that my idea sounds good, but she copies me and does it, too. Except hers doesn't turn out the same because she holds her marshmallows too close to the fire and they burn. "This is stupid," she says. She tries again and still her marshmallows end up crispy and dark like charcoal. "I'm just going to eat the chocolate and graham crackers," she says.

KiKi says, "Peanut butter was a good idea. What else would be good? I want to make another one."

"I was thinking banana slices," I say. "We should put them on the graham cracker, then the chocolate, then the marshmallow." We walk back over to the table and pick out our ingredients. Once we finish making them we join Amanda, who is saving our places on one of the log benches.

Red sits down with us, and a mess of graham cracker crumbs falls to her lap. The four of us are quiet, just sitting and watching the flames of the fire dance.

Red says, "I, um, I wanted to apologize."

None of us say anything.

"I just didn't want to get in trouble," Red says.

Like any of us did.

"But I shouldn't have lied. And just so you know, I did tell Ms. Howard and my parents the truth."

I don't ask Red if she's on punishment, too, but I sure hope she is.

Amanda says, "Apology accepted."

124

KiKi seems hesitant but says, "Same here."

KiKi and Amanda walk over to the cooler to get something to drink.

Red turns to me and says, "And I'm really sorry for how I treated you at Amanda's birthday party."

I'm still kind of mad at Red, but I know the word *sorry* is not easy to say. It can get stuck in your throat like dry, stale crackers. I can't say I totally forgive her right now, so instead I say, "Thank you for apologizing."

Katie comes over to us, asks Red if she wants to make another s'more. Red and Katie walk over to the table and load their sticks with marshmallows. Katie is pretty good at roasting, but Red is getting frustrated. "I don't know why mine keeps burning!" Bobby offers to switch with her because he likes his burned and his just got started. Red tries again, and I can tell she's going to burn them—again—so I walk over to her. I still haven't come up with my third act of kindness, so I think maybe I can help Red. Lizzy said it could be something small. I take Red's hand

and guide it back away from the flame just a bit. Then I move her wrist slowly, side to side, to even out the roasting.

After a while, she starts doing it on her own and the edges of the white puffs turn brown. "There," I say. "They should taste perfect now."

"Thank you," Red says.

"What's your special ingredient going to be?" I ask. "Do you want peanut butter or Nutella? Or what about caramel?"

Red chooses caramel, and I hold her marshmallow stick while she spreads the graham cracker with the gooey goodness and adds the chocolate bar. She takes a bite and says, "I've never tried caramel. This is the best. The. Best."

Deacon LeRoy, Ms. Howard, and Ms. Lee stand and get everyone's attention. They make announcements about what needs to happen in the morning and then they acknowledge all of the youth counselors with a certificate and all the cabin captains with a special button. "Just a little something to thank you for your leadership."

I pin my button on and take in all the applause.

Once we're finished with our dessert, we head back to the cabin as a full group, all of us campers walking up the trail together. It starts to rain, not a storm but a light drizzle. Lizzy says, "I didn't know it was supposed to rain. It's kind of refreshing, though. The night is full of surprises."

Most of the girls rush back to the cabins, but I take my time walking and thinking how I can't wait to show my captain button to Mom and Dad and tell them how I lived up to my name.

15

There's No Place Like Home

THE FIRST PERSON I see when the bus pulls up to the church is Dad. The parking lot is crowded with adults waiting outside their cars, but they are all a blur in the background because Dad is who I am focused on. I lean over KiKi and get closer to the window so I can wave. Dad smiles and waves back at me.

We get off the bus, and Dad walks over and gives me a hug. He hugs Ray, too, and says, "It feels like you two have been gone for a whole year." He walks over to the bus driver, who is unloading our luggage. "Let me help you," Dad says. We wait till Dad has all the bags on the sidewalk and then we're ready to go home. I hug Amanda real tight because I know I won't see her until after I'm off punishment. KiKi and Amanda hug, too.

"Bye, Red," I say. I wave to her.

"Bye."

Ray comes over to me and Dad, and we get in the car. We're just a block away from the church when Dad shouts, "Arizona!"

We all play along.

Dad lies down for a few hours before he leaves for work. Ray and I spend the evening telling Mom all about our time at camp. We talk about the games we played and all the Bible stories we learned. "And I hear you got some practice in apologizing," Mom says. She doesn't sound as disappointed as she did on the phone. "Ryan, did you make things right with Deacon LeRoy and Ms. Howard?"

"Yes."

"Well, good. I know you were just having fun.

Pranks are a part of camp, but I think it went a little too far."

"Ray never said sorry. He started the whole thing," I tell Mom. Ray was there when Aiden and Logan apologized but technically, he didn't say anything.

Mom gives Ray a look. It's the look we get when she wants us to stop playing around, the look that says she is being serious and wants us to do better.

"But Mom—"

"Fix it, Ray. You know what you need to do."

I am not trying to get Ray in trouble, but if I have to be on punishment, he has to at least admit that he was the one who did the first prank.

"I'm sorry, Ryan. I was just trying to have fun."

Mom gets up and goes to the kitchen. "Well, it's time for dinner. Your grandma made a big pot of spaghetti for us."

While she's in the kitchen warming up the pasta and the garlic bread, Ray says, "For real, Ryan. I'm sorry."

"I accept your apology," I tell Ray.

The three of us sit around the table eating dinner. Mom says, "I wanted us to do something special tonight."

I am surprised she says this because I am on punishment and special things don't usually happen when I'm getting a consequence.

"I want the two of you to help me and your dad come up with a name for your baby sister." Mom takes a piece of garlic bread from the center of the table and sets it on her plate. "Your father and I have come up with a few names. And we want your input. All of these names mean something special, but we're just not sure which one is the best one."

"Will it be a name that starts with R?" Ray asks.

"Yes. We've narrowed it down to Ruby, which is a precious jewel, Rochelle, which means 'like a rock,' and Robin, which means 'illuminating light.'"

"I like Ruby," Ray says, and takes another bite of spaghetti.

My mouth is full, so I don't say anything.

Mom looks at me. "And what do you think?"

I take my time to swallow, then say, "I don't know.
I think we should keep brainstorming."

"You don't like any of the names?"

I shrug. "They're okay. I guess Ruby isn't so bad."

"Hmm." Mom eats her bread. "Well, if you come up with a name to put on the list, I'm all ears."

"Really? I can think up a name?"

"Of course. We'll consider it. I don't know that we'll chose it. I kind of like Robin the most."

"That's a type of bird," Ray says.

I laugh.

"I can't believe my own children—who I named—don't like the names I've chosen." Mom shakes her head, a smile spreading across her face.

Since I can't go anywhere, I'll have plenty of time to think about it this week.

I tell Ray and Mom, "I'll come up with something good."

NAMING HER

16

BEING ON PUNISHMENT ISN'T too bad because it's been raining all week, so I haven't wanted to go outside anyway, but I do miss having KiKi and Amanda come over. I spend my days reading so I can complete all the tasks on my Summer Reading Challenge bingo sheets. Yesterday, I finished a row because the last square said *Read Aloud to a Loved One*, and I've been reading to Mom and my baby sister, whose name might be Ruby.

I start a new row today. On the top it says *Read a Book You've Read Before*. Under that square, it says *Read in Your Pajamas*, so I stay in bed and read until

Mom calls me for breakfast. I eat quick and rush back to my room.

By the afternoon, I am making a list of baby names in my notebook. I have a long list and my top three are Ria, River, and Riley. I walk across the hallway to Ray's room. "Ray, I have something to show you."

He opens the door, lets me in. His room has more clutter than mine, but still everything has its place. Dad calls it organized chaos. Mom calls it a mess.

"What do you think of these?" I hand Ray my notebook with my three favorite names circled on top.

"Ria? No. River—really? Riley, maybe."

"Well, they're better than Ruby."

"Why don't you like Ruby? It's the name of a jewel. It represents beauty."

When Ray says this, I get an idea for a name but I don't say it out loud. I just run back to my room so I can write it down.

"That's it?" Ray calls out.

"I have another idea. But I want to wait to tell

everyone all at once." I close my door, sit at my desk, and write it down.

Rose.

It's Sunday, and Dad is home all day. We are outside in the front of the house. Ray is riding his scooter back and forth on the sidewalk and along the walkway. I am sitting on the porch with Mom and Dad, blowing bubbles. Today's heat has faded into a cool breeze, and the sky is changing to evening.

I'm still getting used to our new (old) house, but I like the porch. I like being outside and watching people go by. "Mom, Dad? I have a name for the baby."

"I thought we settled on Ruby?" Dad says.

"No, remember, I told you Ryan had other ideas." Dad nods as if he remembers, but I don't think he does.

Ray stops riding his scooter. He stands with one foot on the scooter, one on the cement. "So, what's the name?"

"Rose," I say.

"Like, my sister's name—your aunt Rose?" Mom asks.

"That's going to be confusing," Ray says. "Two people named Rose in the same family."

"No it won't. Fathers do it all the time. Dad has the same name as Grandpa."

Ray says, "But Ruby represents beauty. She should have a beautiful name."

"Roses are beautiful," I say. "And Grandma says roses have thorns, or really prickles, and that sometimes people think thorns are bad, but really thorns are about survival. They protect the rose, help it keep its beauty."

When I say this, Mom leans forward just a bit and Dad seems more interested.

I have been thinking about how Mom and Dad tell us to be who they named us to be, and all the things Grandma has taught me about beauty, that it isn't about how you look but how you act, how you treat people. I have been thinking that my little sister will need to know how to take care of all the good qualities she'll have, how she'll need to know how to stand up for herself, how beauty will be her strength, her power.

DADDY-DAUGHTER DAYS

IT'S ALREADY THE MIDDLE of August, and soon we'll be going back to school. This summer hasn't been like any other summer, but it hasn't been too bad. Since Mom is still on bed rest and Dad has to sleep during the day, I've been spending a lot of time at Grandma's. She gives me an allowance for helping in her garden and for doing chores around her house.

Love is blooming in Grandma's front yard. Just like she promised, the marigolds she planted in the spring are bursting out of the ground. The yellow, red, and orange flowers lead the way to the back-yard, where we are tending to Grandma's vegetable garden. "Today, we're getting ready for our fall bounty. You know what that means, right?" Grandma asks.

I try to remember the fall greens that Grandma likes. "Um . . . kale, spinach . . ."

"And collards! Got to have my collards."

We start planting, and even though the marigolds are proof that Grandma knows how make things grow, still, I can't believe so much will come from this tiny, tiny seed. As we work, Grandma sings and talks to the soil, and when we are all finished planting and are walking back to the front of the house, Grandma talks to her marigolds. Then she says to me, "You have to nurture the things you want to grow."

I start singing with Grandma, leaning into the flowers like they are microphones. I am so into our song, I don't even realize Dad is here. He's come to pick me up so we can go to the library. I am finally finished with my Summer Reading Challenge and ready to turn in my sheets and pick up my prize.

Grandma wipes her hands on her apron, then digs into her pocket. "You're the perfect little helper," she says. She tucks money into the palm of my hand and kisses me on my forehead.

"I'll bring her back next weekend," Dad says.

Grandma says, "I hope that's a promise."

And we leave.

When we get into the car Dad says, "Before we head to the library, I need to make a stop."

"Where are we going?" I ask.

"Downtown. Your mom made more wallets, purses, and tote bags for Millie to sell at Saturday Market. I need to drop them off."

"Can we stop by Ms. Laura's booth? It won't take me long. I know exactly what I'm looking for."

Dad says yes and after circling the blocks, round and round, we find a space to park. Dad takes out a box from the trunk and we walk over to Millie. Just walking through the crowds of people makes me miss being here every weekend. Maybe I can convince Dad to stop by the concession stand and get a snow cone or an elephant ear on our way back to the car.

We drop the new products off to Millie, who is so glad to see me she hugs me long with an extra squeeze before she lets go. "Give your mom my love," she says to me. She hands Dad an envelope and says, "She sold out of everything. Her summer knits are a hit."

Dad takes the envelope, takes the cash out, and puts it in his wallet. "Thank you so much for selling her items. We need every penny we can get."

"My pleasure, my pleasure." Millie smiles and gives me one more hug before we leave.

I lead the way to Ms. Laura's booth and once we get there, I go straight to the table where the hairpin should be.

It's not there.

"Well, sweetheart, someone must have purchased it," Dad says.

I can't believe I finally have the money to get it and now it's gone. Just as we are about to walk away, Ms. Laura walks over and says hello. She reaches under the table and pulls out a small velvet pouch. "I had a feeling you'd be back for this," she says. She hands me the pouch and when I open it, there it is. The vintage hairpin.

Dad says, "What do we owe you?" and reaches for his wallet.

"Dad, I'm going to pay for it with the money Grandma gave me."

"You keep that for something else. I got this." Dad pays for the hairpin.

"Thanks for saving it for me, Ms. Laura. I can't wait to add it to the others," I tell her.

"And maybe one day you'll wear it in your hair when you have a special occasion," she says. A customer interrupts, asking for help. We say goodbye so Ms. Laura can get back to work. "You all take care. Tell your mom I said hello."

"I will," I say. Before Dad and I walk back to the car I give him the biggest hug I can. Squeeze him tighter than Millie did to me. He squeezes back and I promise, Dad's hugs are the best hugs. We walk to the car, me holding on to the pouch's strings, making sure I don't drop it. I think about asking to stop at the concession stand for my usual Saturday Market treats, but I know Dad won't let me pay and I know Dad has already spent money he didn't have to spend. "Thank you, Dad," I tell him.

"Anything for you," he says.

Our next stop is the library. The first thing I do is look for Ms. Adair so I can show her my bingo sheets. "My, my, my. You sure have been reading. This is fantastic, Ryan." She pulls her keychain from around her neck and says, "I'll be right back with some special prizes for you." She disappears upstairs, and while she's away, I look through the shelves with Dad.

"What's on your list today?" Dad asks.

"Cookbooks," I say. I usually make up my own recipes, but I think it would be good to try out ones that are already perfect because they've been tested. With the baby coming soon, I want to be able to cook more to help out. Even though Grandma and Aunt Rose will be over all the time and probably won't let me do anything but the simple prep work. Maybe we can use the cookbooks and try out recipes together.

"Let's look over here," Dad says. There's a whole section of cookbooks for young chefs, and I want to check all of them out. But that's a whole lot of cooking, so I decide to just get two. One is for meals and the other is only for desserts. Dad and I look through the dessert cookbook and point out the ones we want to make first. "The coconut cream pie is a must," he says.

"And the strawberry mousse, too." I point to the photo and imagine how good it would smell if it was a scratch-and-sniff sticker. I turn the page. "And this looks so good, too," I say, pointing to the walnut mint brownies. "This is going to be so fun."

Ms. Adair is back and is carrying my prize. "Since you have every box marked off, you get four movie passes with free popcorn included, and a gift card to Alberta Street Books."

"Thank you." I put the cookbooks on the counter and hand my library card to Ms. Adair.

"Let me know if you need a taste tester for your new dishes," she says.

I smile.

"And tell your mom hello for me."

"I will."

Dad says goodbye and thanks Ms. Adair. We drive home and we don't play the license plate game because I am looking through the dessert cookbook,

picking out the recipe I'm going to try first. There are so many to choose from. So, so many.

I spend the week trying out new recipes from the cookbooks I checked out.

Today is Dad's day off, and we are spending the whole day together. Ray and Mom are at the house hanging out. Ray is teaching her how to play his favorite video game. Mom is usually the one who does book shopping with me, but Dad isn't so bad. Our first outing is to Alberta Books so I can use my gift card to purchase the cookbooks I checked out from the library. Now that I've tested some of the recipes, I know I will use the books over and over to help with my experiments in the kitchen.

After we leave the bookstore, we go to Fred Meyer to get all the ingredients we need to make no-bake muffins. It's a recipe I've been wanting to try. I have saved every dollar Grandma gave me, so I don't have to ask Dad or Mom for anything.

Dad says, "No-bake muffins?" and he sounds like Ray, who is always leery of what I am making.

"Yes, they're made from instant oatmeal, bananas, shredded coconut, and walnuts. I'm going to top them with a dollop of almond butter."

Dad doesn't look too excited about these.

"They're healthy *and* tasty, and once I put them in the muffin tins to set, they'll come out looking like cute muffin tarts. Well, that's what the picture shows."

"My little chef in the making," Dad says. We walk around the store, filling up the shopping cart. Dad says, "So, tell me more about church camp. Your mom told me about the shenanigans and all, but how was everything else? What did you learn?"

I tell Dad the story of the Good Samaritan and the skit we did, and then I remember that I still haven't done everything on my list. "I haven't done number one yet, and I really want to do it before school starts."

"What is it you want to do?"

"I want to feed the people who sit outside downtown, asking for food." I push the cart down the aisle on the way to the checkout stands and then say to

Dad, "What if I make the muffins for them?" I turn away from the registers and head to the other side of the store that doesn't have groceries. I find the aisle that has greeting cards and gift bags. "See, these would be big enough." I hold up brown paper bags. They are the perfect size. "Maybe I'll decorate the bags or write a little note on them." I realize I am planning and planning but haven't asked for permission yet. "Can I do this, Dad?"

Dad doesn't answer right away but then says, "Ryan, that's a really generous thing to do. Sounds like a great plan."

I have just enough money for everything in the cart. I can't wait to tell Grandma what I purchased with the allowance she gave me.

We get in line, bag our groceries, and get into the car to head home. As we drive down Interstate Avenue, I say to Dad, "So, I think maybe KiKi and Amanda will want to come. We'll have to pick a Sunday when you're off so you can take us."

Dad smiles. "You've got it all figured out, huh?"

Mom comes over to the table and whispers to me, KiKi, and Amanda. "Well, your grandma has a birthday coming up this fall, and we're going to have a big birthday bash for her. I'm inviting relatives from out of town and friends from church. It's going to be a night to celebrate her and tell her how much she means to us all. But . . . it's a secret," Mom says. "You have to promise to keep it between us for now."

I stand up and take the muffins out of the fridge. We wrap the muffins and make an assembly line so we can pack the bags.

"Do you really want us to make the desserts?" I ask.

"Of course," Mom says. "And you can help me cook Grandma's favorite dish for the family dinner."

I can't wait to surprise Grandma and cook with Mom.

Dad comes in the kitchen. "Girls, are you ready? We should get going." He kisses Mom, and we say goodbye.

18

GO AND DO THE SAME

IT IS THE LAST weekend before school starts, and Dad is keeping his promise to take me downtown to feed the homeless. KiKi and Amanda are coming, too. They are with me in the kitchen. We've just finished making no-bake muffins and have to wait for two hours before we can take them out of the muffin tins. While we wait, we decorate the brown paper bags. There are twenty-four muffins, so we prep enough bags for each one.

When Amanda told her mom what we were doing, she sent over sandwiches that we can give out, too. KiKi's mom bought a big bag of tangerines. They are my favorite because they are small and easy to peel.

So now each person will get a sandwich and a tangerine. Amanda says, "Um, Ryan, I need to apologize for something."

I have no idea what Amanda is goi[ng] because I'm not even upset with her about

Amanda says, "I'm sorry for not thinkin[g] it was okay to invite Red to church camp."

KiKi shrugs. "Apology accepted."

I say, "Yes, apology accepted."

KiKi says, "I actually don't mind if Red h with us sometimes."

Amanda looks at me, like she wants to KiKi is speaking for only herself or if I agree

"Not *all* the time, but sometimes, maybe."

Mom comes into the kitchen and says ladies, I am loving what I'm seeing. These ba lovely, and I'm so glad you all took the initiativ this." She opens the fridge and takes out a of water. "These muffins are looking good might need to hire you all to make some do for a special event I'm planning," Mom says.

"What special event?" I ask.

We drive downtown, and as we look for a place to park, KiKi says, "What if there's no one to help?"

Dad pulls over, parks, and says, "There will always be someone to help."

We get out of the car, and at first there are no people to give the bags to. Maybe KiKi was right. I think that's good. If we have to take all these bags home because no one is in need, I'll be happy. But then we turn the corner, and on both sides of the street there are people sitting on the ground with signs and paper cups in front of them asking for money, for food.

Dad is carrying all of the bags in one big tote. We walk over to a woman, and Dad says, "Hello, ma'am, I have a snack bag that my daughter and her friends put together. Would you like one? It was made with love."

The woman looks at us and says, "Is it free?"

"Yes," I say.

She holds her hand out and opens it. "Bless you, bless you."

We keep walking down the block, and we lose track of time giving out the bags.

We have handed them out to men and women, and one person looked like he was the same age as Lizzy and the other college youth counselors. We only have two bags left. It's KiKi's turn to hand one out. When Dad approaches the man sitting at

the corner, he says, "Oh, no thank you." And so we keep walking. We walk toward the car, and I am thinking that we will be taking two bags back to the house, but before we make it back to the car, we see a man walking toward us. "Are you the people giving away food?"

"Yes," Dad says.

"Can I, um, do you have anything left?"

KiKi reaches in the tote and pulls out both bags.

"You can have these."

"Thank you, thank you . . ."

We walk away, and the man is still saying thank you. I look back, and already he is eating one of the sandwiches.

When we get in the car, we don't do a whole lot of talking. We just ride back to the house. When I get home, I'm going to ask Grandma if she has more chores for me to do, because I'll need more money for groceries so we can make something else and do this again.

19

BACK TO SCHOOL

IT'S THE FIRST DAY of school, and the best part is that me and KiKi are in the same class. Hannah Wilkerson is here, too, and her seat is right next to mine. So far, the only not-so-good thing is that Brandon is in my class and we are at the same table group. I wish my desk were next to KiKi's. But instead, she is sitting far away at a table with Marcus and two people I've never had class with before.

My new teacher's name is Ms. Anderson. She is a wide woman, all dressed up like she is going someplace important, and it makes me wonder if teachers care about their back-to-school outfits as much as we do. I expect us to start class sharing about our summer break, and I think I will raise my hand to go first but instead, Ms. Anderson has us go around and say our name and one thing we are good at. After we all have a turn, she passes out thick rectangle-shaped name tags, bigger than any others I've seen. We each get one and our names are printed on the paper, with lots of space inside the letters. "You're going to decorate your name tags, and I'll get these laminated and they'll be on your desk all school year." Ms. Anderson holds hers up as an example. "I want you to be thoughtful about the colors you use, the designs you make. This should represent you—your favorite colors, shapes, and so on. You can even include words that describe you. Make the background something special, too."

I look at Ms. Anderson's name tag. She's got polka dots in one letter, stripes in the next, then polka dots, then stripes. Her colors are purple and white. The background is a bright yellow.

There are small buckets of art supplies in the

center of our table groups. When we start decorating our name tags, Brandon gets going on the same corny jokes he's been saying ever since first grade. "Ryan is a boy's name, and she spells her last name wrong," he says to no one.

I ignore him.

"Hi, Ryan *Heart*break . . . Ryan *Heart* Attack . . . Ryan *Heart*burn . . . Ryan *Heart*beat . . ."

He goes on and on sounding like a parakeet that talks too much.

And the worst one: "Ryan Artichoke Heart."

Already I like Ms. Anderson because she comes over to our desks and asks Brandon, "Are you finished?" and it is the kind of question we all know the answer to without even looking at his paper. Ms. Anderson says, "Stop talking and get back to work."

Once the classroom is working quietly, Ms. Anderson turns on music and there are no words, just instruments, so no one can get distracted by singing along. We just listen while we work and the room is calm and we swap art supplies and take sneak peeks at each other's art. I really like the way mine turned out.

Ms. Anderson collects our name tags, promising that they will be ready tomorrow morning when we come back to class. I think maybe now she will ask us to share what we did this summer, but she doesn't.

We talk about what we'll learn this school year, we talk about the community agreements for using the independent reading bookshelf, and we talk about the new time for lunch and recess. All this talking and nothing about summer.

We go to lunch and recess, and still nothing about summer.

The school day will be ending soon. Finally, just after a short writing lesson, Ms. Anderson says, "I'd like to end the day with a little getting-to-know-you activity. At your table groups, I'd like you to share a special memory you have."

Before she finishes, I blurt out, "A favorite memory from summer?"

"It doesn't have to be from this past summer. Anything that you can remember, from any age, any season," she explains. "Something that was special to you, or funny. It can even be a sad memory.... anything you feel comfortable sharing." And then she steps close to me and whispers, "And next time raise your hand."

Hannah talks about singing in a musical with Oregon Children's Theater. Brandon remembers the first time his family got a new puppy, how every time he comes home, the puppy runs to him and doesn't want to leave his side. I want to ask what the dog's name is, but I don't even want to get Brandon started about names.

It's my turn, and I say, "My memory is about my dad. We don't usually spend a lot of time together, but this summer we did." I tell them all about our trip to the library, and bookstore, and grocery store, and how even though these were just simple outings, they were really special to me.

Ms. Anderson gets our attention and says, "I loved

walking around hearing all these precious memories." She walks through the classroom, giving each of us a sentence strip and a marker. "I want to honor the stories you bring with you when you step into my classroom. We're going to make a memory wall," she tells us. "I'd like you to write your memory down, beginning with the statement *I remember . . .*" Ms. Anderson shows us her example. It is one short sentence and written big enough to see from far away. *I remember fishing on Sauvie Island with my grandpa.*

We practice our sentences on a scratch piece of paper first, and Ms. Anderson comes around our desks to check them before we write the memory on the sentence strip. On my scratch paper, I write a few sentences: *I remember reading cookbooks with my dad.* And then, *I remember riding rides at Oaks Park with my dad.*

It's hard to choose. I raise my hand, tell Ms. Anderson that I'm stuck. "I want to write about one of the memories with my dad, but I don't know which one to choose."

Ms. Anderson says, "Choose the one that you wish could happen again and again."

I want to make sure that what I want to write is okay, but I don't want Brandon to say something silly, so I whisper my sentence in Ms. Anderson's ear. "Is that okay?"

"I think it's perfect," Ms. Anderson says.

I use a green marker to write my sentence. After we've all finished our sentence strips, Ms. Anderson calls us over to the memory wall and tapes them up. Mine is in the middle.

I remember getting tight, warm hugs from my dad.

What Fall Brings

20

THE LEAVES ARE CHANGING and falling like snow-flakes. It's not cold yet, but Mom makes me wear a sweater or light jacket every time I go outside. September went by fast, and school doesn't feel new anymore. It's the middle of October, and Halloween is just two weeks away. I've been thinking of my costume all month: a chef. Grandma is making me an apron with my name on it, and Aunt Rose says she thinks she knows where to buy a chef hat, so I can really look like a top chef.

Since I'm going to be a chef for Halloween, I am trying out new cookie recipes from my cookbook so

I can make a dessert for the harvest festival at church. There's always a dessert contest, and I want to enter this year. I want it to be perfect, so Dad is helping me practice. He's really good at drawing, so he's going to teach me how to decorate the cookies so they look like Halloween cookies and not just sugar cookies with a splatter of icing on them.

Mom calls out to Dad, asking for him to come to the living room.

"Hold on, just a minute," Dad says. "Our daughter is schooling me on how to bake cookies from scratch, and I'm teaching her how to—"

"I can't wait. I need you now," Mom shouts.

Dad rushes into the living room. I follow him.

"It's time to go to the hospital," Mom says. "The baby is coming."

I jump up and down, then run to tell Ray.

By the time I get back to the living room, Dad is already walking Mom to the car. "Aunt Rose will be coming to stay with you. She'll be here as soon as she can," Dad says. That's been the plan since we found out Mom was expecting. Aunt Rose will watch us until Mom and Dad come home from the hospital.

Ray and I wave goodbye, and we stand on the porch watching Dad drive away. We don't go back inside until the car is out of sight.

I walk into the kitchen, looking at the almost-dessert.

Ray asks, "What are you making?"

"I was going to bake sugar cookies."

"Sugar cookies are my favorite."

"Well, too bad we can't have any tonight." I start to put the ingredients away.

"You already have everything ready. And once Aunt Rose is here, it'll be okay to have the oven on."

"I know," I tell him.

"Then why are you looking so sad? You can do it by yourself, right?"

"That's not the point. I wanted Dad to bake with me because he was going to teach me how to decorate them. No one ever cooks with me anymore. Mom always has to rest, and Dad is always asleep or gone," I say.

My back is to Ray, so I don't realize that he is still standing there until he walks over to the sink. He washes his hands. "I'll bake with you."

I don't think Ray has ever, ever made anything except a bowl of cereal and a peanut butter and jelly sandwich. "You will?"

"Yep. And I can practice with you on the decorating—no promises that they'll come out looking gourmet."

"That's okay. It's just practice."

The doorbell rings. Ray lets Aunt Rose in, and she is talking fast and asking all kinds of questions. "Any updates? Have they called?"

"Nothing yet," I tell her.

Aunt Rose gets settled and then she joins us in the kitchen. We follow the recipe, taking turns with the instructions. After the cookies bake, Ray tries to eat one but I won't let him. "They have to cool, Ray. And then we have to decorate them. It's going to be a while."

"How long is a while?" Ray asks.

"I don't know . . . whenever they're ready."

I don't know which is worse, waiting for an update about my baby sister or waiting for the cookies to be done. To pass time, we watch a movie.

When the movie is over, Ray and I go back to the kitchen and decorate the cookies. The first few we do look horrible, but then I get the hang of how hard to squeeze the pastry bags and Ray is figuring out how to mix colors to get the exact tone he wants.

We eat more cookies than Mom or Dad would ever allow. Aunt Rose tells us stories about when we were born and how we acted when we were babies. I love hearing her memories, how her whole face is nothing but love as she talks. "And, Ray, you loved being a big brother," Aunt Rose says. "You two would have full-on conversations. Ray talking in two-year-old sentences, and Ryan responding with gibberish as if you were really talking back to him."

We are finished with our cookies and there is still no update from Dad. Grandma calls to say she is on her way to the hospital, so I think maybe once she is there, she will let us know how Mom is doing. We watch another movie, but I don't make it to the end. I fall asleep midway, so Aunt Rose tells me to get in my pajamas and go to bed. I want to stay up till we hear from Dad or Grandma, until I know I have a baby sister, but my eyes won't stay open. I go to bed, wishing and hoping I'll get to hold her soon.

I wake up at six o'clock in the morning because the phone is ringing and no one is answering it. Aunt Rose is knocked out on the sofa, and Ray is snoring in his room. "Hello?"

"Well hello, big sister," Dad says.

"She's here? She's here?"

"She is. And she is beautiful, and she can't wait to meet you," Dad says. "And one day, you'll tell her that you are the one who named her."

"Rose? You picked Rose to be her name?"

"Yes. Baby Rose is here. Tell your aunt I'll call her later."

When I hang up the phone, I want to run and

wake up Aunt Rose and Ray and tell them the good news. But it is early, and I don't want to interrupt their sleep. I try to go back to bed, but I can't fall asleep. Too many thoughts are in my head. I take out my art supplies and make something special for Mom and Rose. A sign that says Welcome Home.

21

The Thing about Baby Sisters

The thing nobody told me about being a big sister is that the first time I'd hold the baby, I'd feel scared and happy and excited and worried all at the same time. Nobody told me that the first time my baby sister wrapped her tiny, tiny hand around my index finger, I'd never want to stop holding her hand, never want to let her go. They didn't tell me that I'd stand at her crib just to watch her sleep, sneak to wake her up so I can hold her. I didn't know that when people came over to see her, hold her, that I'd watch them to make sure they are holding her head up the way Mom taught me. Nobody told me that my baby

pictures would look just like her baby pictures, and so everyone in the family calls us twins and can't believe how much we look alike.

The other thing nobody told me is that baby sisters cry and sleep and cry and eat and cry and cry and need their diapers changed and on and on it goes every day, every night. Nobody told me I wouldn't be able to play with her much. Right now, it really doesn't matter that there are three girls in the house because Rose can't talk or do much of anything, so when we take a family vote on what to have for dinner or what movie to watch on movie night, Rose is not much help. But she will be. I know it because $2 + 1 = 3$ and *1 brother + 2 sisters = more girls* and *1 dad + 1 brother + 1 mom + 2 sisters = more girls.* So one day, one day, baby Rose will team up with me and Mom and we will win votes about which ride to get on at Oaks Park, and we will beat them in water balloon fights, and one day I will tell her about her beginning.

Already, I am her favorite. I can tell. Like yesterday

when Mom was giving her a bath. Rose was holler-ing the whole time until I came in and sang to her while Mom finished drying her and getting her dressed for the day.

And right now, we have already said our good nights and all the lights are off, except my night-light, and Dad is gone, and Ray is snoring, and Rose is crying. I can hear Mom pacing back and forth; the floors are creaking and crying, too.

I get out of bed and go to Mom's room.

"Ryan? Sweetheart, sorry we woke you. Go back to bed, everything's okay." Mom says this when it is very clear that nothing is okay. She is bouncing Rose and rocking her and walking around her room look-ing tired and frustrated. The lamp is on, but mostly the room is dark.

"Can I hold her?"

"She's too fussy right now. I'm trying to get her to go to sleep." Mom puts the pacifier back in Rose's mouth. It won't stay because Rose's mouth is wide open in a full-on scream.

I sit in the armchair and hold my arms out. "Let me try," I say.

Mom gives in. As she walks over to me, I sit up straight, propped up against the square pillow. Mom places Rose in my arms, handing her over to me like she is a delicate wish. I hold Rose close to me and whisper, "Shh . . . shh . . . don't cry . . . it's okay."

Mom sits on her bed, yawning and rubbing her eyes.

"Shh . . . shh . . . don't cry . . . it's okay."

Rose cries and cries, but finally, after I rock her and whisper to her and hold her close, she falls asleep. And Mom does, too. I lean forward to get up so I can lay Rose down in her crib, but she starts whimpering, so I lean back and rock her some more. "Shh . . . shh . . . don't cry . . . it's okay."

I sit very still so Rose doesn't wake up. I watch her smile while she's sleeping and wonder what she's dreaming of.

MAKING MEMORIES

22

TODAY AT SCHOOL A new student joined our class, and Ms. Anderson asked me to explain the memory wall activity to her. I helped her tape her statement on the wall, and we stood and read the whole wall together. When I told Ms. Anderson that I wish I could add more, she said I could always make my own lists in a journal.

So tonight, after dinner and before I go to bed, I write down all of the special memories I can think of. Especially ones from this past summer, because those are extra special since I didn't think I would have any fun or do any of the traditions that Mom and I usually do.

My list is long and still there's more to say. Good thing I have plenty of paper left in this notebook. When Mom walks by my bedroom for the final lights-out call, I put my journal on my dresser next to the mystery canister. I know it's time for bed, but I just want to look inside one more time: two seashells, a postcard addressed to no one, a white handkerchief embroidered with purple flowers, dried rose petals, and now there are four gold hairpins.

I've always thought these things were too simple to cherish, but I wonder if they were saved because a teacher asked, *What are your special memories?* Maybe this a way to remember the little things, the things that don't seem so special at first but then turn out be the best thing.

"Ryan! Lights out," Mom calls one more time.

I turn the light off, rush over to my bed. I fall asleep thinking maybe I'll keep making these lists in my journal and maybe I'll ask Mom if there's an old canister or container I can have so I can start my own keepsake box. I have so many memories I want to hold on to, so many more to make.

ACKNOWLEDGMENTS

Sometimes I don't realize the stories I carry with me until I start writing, and then I hear the church songs taught to me at Vacation Bible School, feel Ms. Tiny's fingers braiding my hair, smell the roses in my grandmother's garden. It all comes back, and I am reminded of how much laughter I had with Akiba, Karen, Clarvetta, and Tanisha at sleepovers and birthday parties and all the times we got together just because. Though Ryan's story is not my exact story, I do come from a similar loving, supportive family and community. I am so thankful for all of them.

Thank you, Ms. Adair, the librarian who always knew the perfect book to recommend. You are no longer here with us, but your legacy lives on in all the young readers you nurtured.

Thank you to my mother, Carrie Watson, to Grandma Roberta, Aunt Mary, and Ms. Fisher, Ms. Celestine, Ms. Walters, and Ms. Simmons for being the chorus of wise women who inspired the women characters in this book.

Thank you to my expert kid readers, Araceli Hagan Flores and Xavier Hertel, for reading early drafts and giving me invaluable feedback.

Thank you, Kori Johnson, Olugbemisola Rhuday-Perkovich, Linda Christensen, and Ellen Hagan—always you cheer me on, ground me, and help me wade through the intimidating revision waters.

Thank you to my team at Bloomsbury, especially my editor, Sarah Shumway, and to my agent, Rosemary Stimola. I appreciate your guidance.

And much love to the *real* Hart family for inspiring these tales.